會賺$的貿易英文

Smart慣用語跟老外 這麼說 ，賺$有效率！

快 賺$的 英文溝通術
供4大Smart吸$招數

- 了解英文慣用語背後的文化秘密 擺脫學習總是死記、一知半解的學習模式。
- 活用慣用語的換句話說 讓職場上的英語溝通與表達更活潑、不呆板！
- 融會貫通英文慣用語 在辦公室溝通、會議、業務採購、國貿工作領域中的用法，實用性、學習效果100%！
- 非學不可的職場小貼示 除了有貼心提醒的know-how外，另有精準剖析的關鍵詞彙，用英語自在地馳騁在工作領域 不出錯！

作者序

　　語言其實就是文化的縮影，從一字詞的挑選與邏輯的組合，都可以看出一個國家甚至文化圈對於人事物的認知。做為中文母語者，當開口就能用上一兩句成語來豐富內容，會給人學識淵博的感受。相同地，英文的慣用語也能表現你對西方文化的諸多認識，讓你的英文更加道地。

　　有鑑於此，此書特以辦公室溝通、辦公室會議、業務採購銷售與國際貿易溝通為主題，挑選31個慣用語，以輕鬆的筆法說明典故，並透過範例對話解釋如何將其套入商用對談中，最後再補充相關商業知識，系統性地增近商用英語能力，讓讀者可以用三言兩語，就開口說好英語。

邱佳翔

編者序

學習語言最有效率的方式，就是從了解目標語言的文化背景；再來就是用對方法。本書除了幫助讀者認識英文慣用語的由來外，更將英文慣用語和職場情境做結合，並於情境對話中模擬公司同仁間、上司與下屬間的多向溝通，讓上班族預先準備好工作上會碰到的各種狀況，也準備好拿出正確的英文來應對。

相信這樣的規劃能有助學習上融會貫通，英文能力提升了，職場競爭力必能一併大躍進，當然就會賺大＄囉！共勉之。

編輯部

Contents 目次

Part 1 【內勤】辦公室溝通篇

Part 2 【內勤】辦公室會議篇

Part 3 【外勤】業務／採購銷售篇

Part 4 【外勤】國際貿易溝通與人事篇

Part 1
【內勤】辦公室溝通篇

Unit 01 Keep somebody posted
有消息／進度請通知

 A 辭彙文化背景介紹

　　Post 有張貼的意思，所以當你第一眼看到keep *sb.* posted這個用法時，可能會直覺想到一直保持張貼狀態到底要有什麼用意。當你這樣想時，其實已經快要找到答案了！

　　如果用現在大家不可或缺的facebook與Instagram做比喻，相信大家一定可以馬上記住這個片語的意思。現在大家習以為常的po文，其實完整的講法是 post an article。那如果對方一Po文你能馬上得知，就意味你可以掌握對方的狀況，講到這邊，其實已經差不多告訴大家這個片語的意思了，這個片語主要就是要表達「有新的消息請讓我知道」。

　　因此，如果你是員工，下次要請同事讓你能夠隨時掌握某項工作的進度，或是你是主管，要求員工讓你知道某個工作的狀況時，都可以說 "Keep me posted"（「有消息請通知我。」）。

看看辭彙怎麼用

【同事間】Between colleagues

Simpson 辛普森	Bart, our proposal is **rejected**. I was a little bit shocked. Does anything go wrong during our briefing?	巴特，我們的企劃案被拒絕了。我有點震驚。簡報時我們有出錯嗎？
Bart 巴特	I guess not. How about checking the power point slides one after one to see if we can find clues?	我覺得沒有耶！不然？不然我們一張一張投影片檢查，看看我們能不能找出點線索呢？
Simpson	Good idea, let's begin with **statistics** and formula. The figures we use in this report are all from the **authorities**, so the chance to be wrong is low. The problem may come from the formula itself.	好主意，就從統計數字跟公式開始看吧！我們的數據都引自權威機構，所以出錯的機會很低，很可能是公司本身出錯。

Bart	Very logical reasoning. Now I **randomly** select an equation to verify. Gosh! One parameter in the calculation of disposable asset is wrong, making the outcome somehow unreasonable. I assume that is reason why ABC Company feel hesitant. I think I should ask Anna to double check all the parameter in case we miss any mistake.	很合邏輯的推斷。現在我隨機選擇一個等式來驗算看看。我的天啊！計算可支配資產中的參數有一個是錯的，讓結果看起來有些不合理。我覺得這就是ABC公司猶豫的原因。我覺得應該要請艾咪再次檢查所有參數，以免再次有所遺漏。
Simpson	It might take Amy few hours to finish this job and I have a meeting with KPL Industry later, <u>so please keep me posted about the verification.</u> Once it has been done, I will ask Mr. Huang, the manager to help us to arrange another presentation for ABC's CEO. See you later.	艾咪檢查可能需要幾小時，而且我等一下要跟KPL工業開會，所以有任何更正請讓我知道，一旦完成檢查，我會請黃經理再幫我們安排跟ABC公司執行長簡報的機會。我就先走了。
Bart	See you later.	再見

【主管與屬下間】

Between the supervisor and the employee

Derrick 得瑞克	How is the progress in the customer development after the trade show last month?	上個月參加展覽後，目前客戶開發的進度如何呢？
Bill 比爾	Now ANB wants us to send the quotation of CNC machine, and Amy updates the progress to me every three days. However, the situation of ETU is not clear. Though they show great interest in our pressing machine in the **exhibition**, we haven't received the response to the quotation we have sent one week ago.	現 在ANB要CNC機器的報價，而艾咪每三天會跟我回報進度。但ETU的狀況有點不明，雖然他們在展覽期間對於壓床機展現高度興趣，但上週給予報價後就音訊全無。
Derrick	I am afraid that some of our competitors tend to use low price as the **incentive** to get this order, so now you get my authorization to negotiate the price. The maximum is 10 percent off, and you make the decision without asking me in this range.	我怕是因為我們的競爭者想以低價作誘因搶訂單，所以於此我授權你議價的權力。上限是九折，所以在這個範圍內的價格，你可以全權作主。

	Considering the scale of ETC, I think it has the potential to be our agent in that region. <u>Please keep me posted if you have any progress.</u>	考量到ETU的規模，它有潛力成為本公司在該地區的代理商。接下來，如有任何進度，請都告訴我。
Bill	I got it. I will firstly write an e-mail to show that we can have some **compromise** in the price to re-initiate the talk.	了解。我會先寫電子郵件告知他們我方願意在價格上讓步，以重啟雙方之對談。
Derrick	Good. Once ETU requests the discount above this range, please let me know. I will tell you whether to accept it or not.	很好。萬一ETU要求比這更多的優惠，請告訴我，我會裁示是否接受。
Bill	I see.	了解。

 對話單字、片語說分明

① **rejected** *v.* 拒絕

　例　The proposal is rejected due to its highly estimated budget.
　　　這個提案由於預估費用過高而被否決。

② **statistics** *n.* 統計數字

例 According to the statistics, our sales figure has made a great improvement this year.

根據統計數字，本年度的銷售數字成長卓著。

③ **authorities** *n.* 當局、權威機構

例 Without the approval from local authorities, this machine can't be imported.

若沒有當局的許可，此機器不能進口。

④ **randomly** *adv.* 隨機地

例 To get the direct feedback from customers, this survey randomly select testees in the mall.

為了獲得顧客最直接的回饋，本調查在賣場中隨機挑選受測者。

⑤ **exhibition** *n.* 展覽

例 To get more brand awareness, we need to put more resources in advertisements.

為了要更提高品牌知名度，得在廣告上投入更多資源。

⑥ **incentive** *n.* 誘因

例 For the high-end consumers, being unique is the greatest incentive that attracts them to purchase this item.

對高端消費者而言，有特殊性是吸引它們購買產品的最大誘因。

⑦ **compromise** *v/n.* 妥協

 Considering the long-term cooperation, we can compromise in this case.

考量到彼此會長期合作，這次我們可以讓步。

D 換句話說補一補

The figures we use in this report are **all from the authorities**, so the chance to be wrong is low.

我們的數據都引自權威機構，所以出錯的機會很低。

★ The figures we use in this report are **all from reliable source**, so the chance to be wrong is low.

★ The figures we use in this report **all have been verified**, so the chance to be wrong is low.

★ The figures we use in this report are **all have the endorsement from the profession**, so the chance to be wrong is low.

 解析時間

① **from a reliable source**

解析 from a reliable source 意思是來源可靠，換言之，也是表達權威機構的公正性。在職場上，我們會接觸到各式各樣的圖表與統計數字，如何讓人對其信服，就是資料的出處。

② **all have been verified**

解析　all have been verified意思是皆經過驗證。能通過驗證，代表有人對其正確度把關，因此也算的上來自權威機構的替代用語。

③ **all have the endorsement from the profession**

解析　all have the endorsement from the profession意思是有專家的背書。換個角度看，也是在表示資料的可靠性。在職場上，為了不損及自身利益，大家對於數據的真實性難免持有懷疑，因此若要取信於人，不妨搬出專家背書這項武器，使用 "The data all have the endorsement from the profession." 這類的句型，好讓對方對安心。

Now I **randomly** select an equation to verify.

現在我隨機選擇一個等式來驗算看看。

★ Now I select an equation **by chance** to verify.

★ Now I select an equation **without specific principle** to verify.

★ Now I select an equation **with my intuition** to verify.

 解析時間

① **by chance**

解析　by chance意思是按照機率。由於沒有設立規則，所以每個樣本被抽到的機率都均等，也就是隨機抽樣的概念。因此，當我們在職場上要表達某件事情其實沒啥規則可言，就可以用 by chance來表示。

② **without specific principles**

解析 without specific principles意思是沒有特別的規則。換言之，唯一的規則就是憑機率，因此也能用來表達隨機抽樣的概念。

③ **with my intuition**

解析 with my intuition意思是憑直覺，在概念上也很接近隨機，因此也可以用來表達隨機抽樣。

I will firstly write an e-mail to show that we can have some **compromise** in

the price to re-initiate the talk.

我會先寫電子郵件告知他們我方願意在價格上讓步，以重啟雙方之對談。

★ I will firstly write an e-mail to show that we can have some **flexibility** in the price to re-initiate the talk.

★ I will firstly write an e-mail to show that we can **give you some favor** in the price to re-initiate the talk.

★ I will firstly write an e-mail to show that we can **have some discounts** to re-initiate the talk.

 解析時間

① **flexibility**

解析 flexibility意思是彈性。在價格上讓步，其實也就是不堅持某個數字。因此，未來當你與客戶協議價格出現僵局時，就可以

用 "the price of..may have some flexibility" 來表達。

② give you some favor

解析 give you some favor意思是給予你一些優惠。在價格上給予優惠，其實也就是些許讓步來加速成交。因此，當你發現客戶遲遲不願下單時，就可以在自己權限內給予折扣，例如 "I can give you some favor"，來縮短成交時程。

③ have some discounts

解析 have some discounts意思是給予折扣。在價格上讓步就是願意給折扣。比起一些複雜的組合方案，直接打折的吸引力最大，因此當你希望客戶快點下單時，就可以用 "you can have some discount if..." 這樣的句型來使其動心。

E 非學不可的職場小貼示

　　Authorization意思是授權。授權的目的在於取得原本自己所沒有的權限。在職場上，長官會視情況釋放部分權力給下屬，以便執行業務。往後如果在執行業務上有需要，就可以用 "To make..., may I have your authorization to..." 這類句型向長官請示，請其給與授權。而如果你自己本身就是長官，則可採用 "here I authorize... to..." 讓下屬可以盡快完成工作。

Unit 02 Touch base / out of touch
把情況告訴某人／不聯絡

 辭彙文化背景介紹

在解釋touch base之前，要先跟大家介紹一下棒球這個運動。如果看過棒球賽或是打過棒球，就會知道壘包叫做base。打者把球擊出後，如果沒有比防守者先碰到壘包，就是出局，換句話說，打者要先碰到壘包，才能繼續在該局比賽或是得分。

因為有這樣的先後順序，後來touch base就衍生出先把情況告訴某人的意思。既然touch有聯繫的意思，out of touch從字面上看，就是超出可聯繫範圍，因而衍生出不聯絡的意涵。

了解兩個片語的典故後，如果往後工作時發現有些事情是要先向某人報告的，記得用I have to touch base with someone about something.這類句型表示。若發現已經斷了聯繫，導致訊息脫節，就可以用I am out of touch with...。

B 看看辭彙怎麼用

【同事間】Between colleagues

Allen 艾倫	Morning, Evans, have you convinced MCX to place the new order? If you can make it, you are the most competitive candidate in **ranking** of the top sales in our company this year.	早安，伊凡斯。你說服MCX下新的訂單了嗎？如果你成功了，你很可能就是今年年度最佳銷售員了。
Evans 伊凡斯	Not yet. Last month the Director of the International Sales Department of MCX, Jonathan quit due to the personal reason, <u>so I have to touch base with the successor to finalize the deal soon.</u>	其實還沒。上個月MCX的國貿經理強納森因為個人因素請辭，所以我必須和繼任的人說明整個情況，以便快點完成交易。
Allen	In this case, you may have few miles to go.	如果是這樣的話，你可能還得加把勁了！
Evans	You are right. Ryan, the new director is relatively **conservative**, making the chance high for MCX to reduce the quantity.	沒錯。新任的經理萊恩相對而言個性比較保守，所以很有可能會減少購買數量。

Allen	Have you found the solution to this problem?	那你有想到什麼對應策略了嗎？
Evans	In order not to be out of touch with any progress of this deal, I have asked Richard to arrange a meeting as soon as possible. I will try my best to get Ryan's signature on the order.	為了不要漏掉本次交易任何進度，我已經請李察盡快安排會面，會盡全力讓萊恩點頭答應。
Allen	Good luck, man.	祝你好運了。
Evans	Thank you. Wait for my good new.	謝謝。等我的好消息。

【主管與屬下間】

Between the supervisor and the employee

Luke 路克	Hey, David, the shipping time is approaching, so I would like to know how's the final test of CNC machine?	嘿，大衛。出貨日快到了，所以我想知道CNC機器的最後測試進度如何？

David
大衛

Almost done, but now we find a **bug**. When keying in the parameters that exactly reach the maximum in size, the software will detect as **invalid** values. I think the reason comes from the coding, so I have asked Jimmy to check the programming in this function.

幾乎都好了，但我們發現一個漏洞。就當輸入與尺寸最大值相同的參數時，軟體會將其判讀為無效值。我想問題應該是出在編碼上，所以已經請吉米檢查此功能的程式內容。

Luke

How long does it take according to you **estimation**? Don't give me the answer like one more week or I will blow up.

你預估這樣的檢查需要多久時間呢？別跟我說還要一個星期之類的話，這樣我真的會發飆。

David

Don't worry, two days at most I promise. I will touch base with you when Jimmy solves the problem.

別擔心，我保證最多就兩天。吉米一把問題解決，我就會告訴你

Luke

I feel much relieved upon hearing this. Since this order is very important to us in this region, we can't afford any mistake.

聽到你這樣說我放心多了。因為這張訂單對在該區的生意舉足輕重，我禁不起出任何差錯。

| David | I know how serious it would be if we mess it up, so I will check all the other details again. | 我知道搞砸的嚴重性，所以會再檢查所有細節一次。 |
| Luke | Good job, David. Dial my extension when you and Jimmy finish the examination. | 做得好。等你跟吉米完成檢查，打分機通知我。 |

C 對話單字、片語說分明

① **ranking** *n.* 排名

例 Mugs are the number one in ranking of our best seller.
馬克杯是我們最暢銷的商品。

② **successor** *n.* 繼任者

例 Since Amy just quit last week, we have to find a successor to her position.
由於艾咪上周辭職，我們得找到她職位的繼任者。

③ **finalize** *v.* 結束

例 To finalize this deal soon, we provide a 10 percent discount.
為了盡快成交，我們給你九折優惠。

④ **conservative** adj. 保守的

例 If the economy is bad, being conservative is not necessarily bad.

經濟狀況如果不佳，保守些也不見得不好。

⑤ **bug** n. 漏洞

例 The system will shut down automatically if any bug is detected.

如有偵測到漏洞，系統會自動停止。

⑥ **invalid** *adj.* 無效的

例 Once you key in the wrong parameter, the signal of "invalid value" will be shown on the panel.

當你鍵入錯誤參數時，面板上會出現「無效值」的訊息。

⑦ **estimation** *n.* 預估

例 The time needed for this task is beyond my estimation, so now I am a little bit behind the schedule.

這項工作所需的時間超出我的預期，所以我現在進度上有點落後。

換句話說補一補

Ryan, the new director is relatively **conservative;** making the chance high for MCX to reduce the quantity.

新任的經理萊恩相對而言個性比較保守,所以很有可能會減少購買數量。

★ Ryan, the new director**has less courage to take risk**, making...

★ Ryan, the new director **tends to do things in moderation**, making...

★ Ryan, the new director **is not that aggressive**, making...

 解析時間

① **has less courage to take risk**

　解析 has less courage to take risk意思是「比較不敢冒險」。換句話說,就是做事比較中規中矩或是保守。在職場上,保守不見得是壞事,特別是在狀況不明的時候。

② **tend to do things in moderation**

　解析 tend to do things in moderation意思是「凡事採中庸之道」。換句話說,就是不會特別消極或積極。在職場上,太愛出鋒頭或是太愛偷懶都會成為同事攻訐的目標,所以搞清楚公司文化之前,給人I do thing in moderation的感覺就比較不會吃虧。

③ **is not that aggressive**

解析 is not that aggressive意思是「不是那麼地有幹勁」。Aggressive在概念上與conservative近乎完全相反，因此not aggressive就可視為保守。在職場上，若聽到同事aggressive形容你的工作態度，可別高興得太早，因為這個單字也隱含某人很有野心，他／她可能是褒中帶貶。

The shipping time is **approaching**, so I would like to know how 's the final test of CNC machine?
出貨日快到了，所以我想知道CNC機器的最後測試進度如何？
★ The shipping time is **around the corner**, so...?
★ The shipping time is **coming**, so...?
★ **Not having much time left before** the shipping time, so...?

 解析時間

① **around the corner**

解析 around the corner單看字面意思，是「要繞過轉角了」，但實際上是根據字面所呈現的空間感引伸出「接近了」的意思。因此，在工作時如果發現某項任務的最後期限快到了，就可以用thedeadline of ... is around the corner來表示。

② **coming**

解析 coming意思是來臨。此用法在概念上最直觀，沒有運用任何比喻。因此在職場上如果要說明活動、會議等舉辦時間已很接

近，就可以用 the meeting/event is coming 來表示。

③ **Not having much time left before....**

(解析) Not having much time left before 意思是離⋯已經沒剩多少時間，是以另一個角度來說明時間已很接近，提醒意味更加濃厚。因此，不論是同事間相互提醒，或是長官告誡下屬時間的急迫性，都可以用 not having much time left before 來表示。

Almost done, but now we find a **bug.**
幾乎都好了，但我們發現一個漏洞。
★ Almost done, but now we find a **loophole**
★ Almost done, but now we find a **flaw**
★ Almost done, but now we find a **weakness**.

 解析時間

① **loophole**

(解析) loophole 的原意是小孔，後來引申為系統、想法中所出現的缺點。因此在職場溝通上，如果發現對方想法有邏輯上的瑕疵，或是系統在設計上出現問題，就分別可以用 the thought may have some loopholes 與 the system may have some loopholes 來表示。

② **flaw**

(解析) flaw 意思是缺陷。缺陷在嚴重程度上又比缺點更高一級，因

為有缺點不見得影響整體，但講到有缺陷，就讓人直接聯想到不處理所產生的嚴重後果。因此在職場溝通上，若你覺得產品的設計就已經出問題，或是概念的架構不恰當，就可以用The design/thought has some flaws來表示。

③ **weakness**

解析 weakness意思是弱點。從資安角度看，系統的弱點就是漏洞所在。從思維邏輯的角度看，想法的弱點就是在架構上有問題。因此當與同事溝通，若發現他／她所提出看法有矛盾或不清楚之處時，就可以用your thought may have some weaknesses if I ....向其說明問題的癥結點。

E 非學不可的職場小貼示

在本單元的對話中，伊凡斯曾說到I will try my best to get Ryan's signature on the order。從字面上看，就是我會讓訂單上有萊恩的簽名。那有了簽名代表什麼意思呢？不論是從貿易面或法律面來看，只要在具備法律效力的文件簽名，只要在當中的簽名處簽名，即代表認可文件內容。了解這層涵義後，以後在職場上聽到Please have your signature on....時，請記得再確認整個文件內容一遍，以免自己的權益受損，或是莫名其妙地得替某事負責。

Unit 03 Hang in there / hang on
再堅持一下

 A 辭彙文化背景介紹

　　Hang 有「懸掛」的意思，所以當第一眼看到 hang in there，應該直覺翻譯為「掛在那裡」。此一用法據傳是 70 年代的激勵標語海報，海報中有隻小貓抓著樹枝。由於只要鬆開爪子，小貓就會掉下去，因此 hang in there 就衍生出「撐下去」的意涵了。

　　本用法的真正典故似乎鮮為人知，但如果用猜字母遊戲 hangman 來聯想，就很容易理解。擔任 hangman 遊戲出題者的人會先畫一個吊桿及列出單字的字母數量（用 _ _ _ _ 來表示），若猜題者猜出正確字母，就填上空格，若猜錯就畫上一筆，錯的次數越多，被吊掛的人形就越完整。當人形全部畫完，猜題者就輸掉遊戲。

　　在玩 hangman 遊戲時，即使出題方略占上風，只要猜題者再努力一下，就有機會贏得遊戲。秉持相同的邏輯，在工作上遭遇困難，不論你是主管還是員工，若要自我激勵或是鼓勵他人，希望大家再加把勁，就可以用 hang in there 這句話來鼓舞工作士氣。

B 看看辭彙怎麼用

【同事間】Between colleagues

Dennis 丹尼斯	Terry, you look **extremely** exhausted. Guess you had a tight schedule during the business trip in USA.	泰瑞，你看起來非常累。我猜你在美國出差的行程很緊湊吧。
Terry 泰瑞	I had **marathon** meetings in the last week because I had to contact with all of our suppliers in this region. What's more, our supplier will invite me to have dinner after the meeting. Thus, I barely have time to rest.	因為必須跟所有美國的供應商接觸，我過去一週都在馬拉松式的開會。此外，開會完供應商都會邀請我共進晚餐，所以我幾乎沒時間休息。
Dennis	Poor you. Are you still in **jet lag** now?	真是辛苦了！你現在還有時差嗎？
Terry	To be honest, yes. I'm **craving for** a few days off, but I can't.	說真的，還有時差。我很想休假但不能。
Dennis	Why? I remember you tell me that you still have 3 PTOs (paid time off) left.	為什麼不能休假呢？我記得你跟我講說你還有三天特休。

Terry	True. However, I have to submit the trip report by this Friday. To keep being awake, I have consumed so much caffeine from this afternoon.	我的確還有特休，但本週五就必須提交出差報告。為了保持清醒，下午開始我就喝了好幾杯咖啡了。
Dennis	Hang in there, dude. You only get two more working days left. Let's have beer to relax this Friday night.	夥伴，撐著點。再工作兩天就可以放假了。星期五晚上一起喝啤酒放鬆吧！
Terry	It sounds great. Now I feel much more energetic. Thank you, buddy.	聽起來很棒，我現在比較有精神了。兄弟，謝謝啦！
Dennis	Not to mention that.	別客氣。

【主管與屬下間】

Between the supervisor and the employee

Josh 喬許	Bad news, guys. Since board of the directors tend to change the investment policy, we have to re-write all the proposals we have finished for next year. It will be an acid test for us because the deadline is two weeks from today.	各位，我這邊有個壞消息。由於董事會打算改變投資政策，所以已經完成的明年度提案都必須重寫。這會是個嚴峻的考驗，因為從今天算起兩週內就必須完成。
Cindy 辛蒂	Oh, it is really a **nightmare**. We spend so much time in those reports, but now it begins from zero again. I'm getting a **headache** now.	喔，真是噩夢一場。這些報告花了我們不知道多少時間，結果現在要重來。我頭好痛。
Mary 瑪莉	Me, too. I have to re-calculate the outcome of the equation for another week.	我也是。我有得花整個星期來計算等式了。
Josh	I know it is so frustrating, <u>but please hang in there</u>. Think of the bright side; it is a good time for us to show our ability to the boss.	我知道這讓人很沮喪，但請各位撐住啊！往好處想，這是向老闆們證明能力的好機會。
Cindy	Maybe you are right. Now I will face the music to begin with the proposal of investment plan in Spain.	或許你是對的。我會面對現實，開始重寫西班牙的投資計畫。

Josh	Good job. To **empathize** your hard working, I treat you coffee today. Which flavor do you want?	做得好。為了體恤你們的辛勞，我請喝咖啡。你們要什麼口味的？
Cindy	Hot black coffee, thank you.	熱黑咖啡，謝謝。
Mary	Iced Latte without sugar, please.	我要冰拿鐵不加糖。

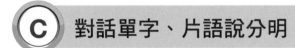

(C) 對話單字、片語說分明

① **extremely** *adv.* 非常地

例 After working overtime for five hours, I am extremely tired.

加班五小時後，我累到不行。

② **marathon** *n.* 馬拉松；*adj.* 馬拉松式的

例 It is a tough task to have a marathon meeting all day long.

一整天馬拉松式的會議是件苦差事。

③ **jet lag** *n.* 時差

例 Please put jet lag into consideration when arranging a meeting, or the foreign attendee may feel listless when discussing.

安排會議時請把時差也列入考慮，否則外國與會人開會時會無精打采。

④ **be craving for....** *ph.* 渴望…

例　With high working pressure for weeks, I am craving for a short vacation now.

由於幾週來工作壓力都很大，我很想現在去度個假。

⑤ **nightmare** *n.* 噩夢

例　Annual auditing is always the nightmare to me.

年度稽核一直都是我的噩夢。

⑥ **headache** *n.* 頭痛；*adj.* 令人頭痛的

例　The customer feedback analysis makes me have a headache.

顧客回饋分析令我頭痛。

⑦ **empathize** *v.* 表達同理心

例　To empathize your hard working, the board of directors decide to offer you a free trip to Japan.

為體恤你的辛勤工作，董事會決定招待你去日本旅遊。

D 換句話說補一補

Thus, I barely **have time** to rest.
所以我幾乎沒時間休息。

★ Thus, I **almost find no time** to rest.
★ Thus, I **find it hard to have** time to rest.
★ Thus, **having enough time to rest is like a mission impossible**.

 解析時間

① **almost find no time**

　解析 almost find no time意思是「幾乎找不出時間」，換句話說，就是能夠利用的時間很少，因此在意涵上與have barely time相近。兩者差別在於本用法更強調「試圖」的語氣。因此下次當你覺得行程很滿或是工作量很大，想騰出時間卻又沒辦法，就可以用I almost find no time to...來發發牢騷。

② **find it hard to...**

　解析 find it hard to...意思是「有困難…」，換個角度看，就是評估過後發現幾乎不可能做到某個標準，或是完成某件事情。在職場上，無法凡事盡如人意，因此當你發現事情的發展無法如你所願時，就可以用I find it hard to...來表達心中的感受。

③ **V-ing enough n. to v. is like a mission impossible**

　解析 having enough time to rest is like mission impossible

意思是「有足夠時間休息根本就是個不可能的任務」，換句話說，就是表達想休息但卻無法做到的無奈。這樣的說法比較輕鬆一些，因此建議同事間發發牢騷時使用，若對象是主管，還是正經一些為宜。

It will be **an acid test** for us because the deadline is two weeks from today.
這會是個嚴峻的考驗，因為從今天算起兩週內就必須完成。
★ It will be **a tough task** for us because...
★ It will be **a fierce challenge** for us because...
★ It will take efforts to accomplish this mission because...

 解析時間

① **a tough task**
　解析　a tough task意思是「不容易完成的事情」，從另個角度，也是一項考驗。Acid test在商業領域中，指的是判斷某間公司是否擁有足夠資產來解決短期負債能力的檢驗，由於這樣測試通常是短期且密集，也確實是件不簡單的，因此下次在工作上遇到困難且有時間壓力的任務，也可以用a tough task來表示。

② **a fierce challenge**
　解析　a fierce challenge意思是「激烈的挑戰」，在概念上與上述用法相近，只是把重點放在如果贏得挑戰，需承擔其後果。根據這樣的邏輯，當我們在工作時，如果碰到那種無法完成就會

倒大楣的任務時，就可以用 a fierce challenge來表示。

③ **It will take efforts to accomplish this mission**

解析 It will take efforts to accomplish this mission意思是「需要一番努力才能完成任務」，主要也是在表達這件事情需要花費很多心力。因此，當我們發現某項工作並不容易完成時，就可以採用本句型。

Think of the bright side; it is a good time for us to show our ability to the boss.
請各位撐住啊！往好處想，這是向老闆們證明能力的好機會。
★ **To see thing in a positive way**, it is a good time...
★ **It's just I like a coin having two sides**; it is a good time...
★ **A crisis is a turning point**, so it is a good time...

 解析時間

① **To see thing a positive way**

解析 To see thing a positive way意思「從正面角度看事情」，與看事情的光明面在語意上其實相當接近，都是要人凡事往好處想。因此，當在工作上遇到困難或挫折，要自我激勵或激勵他人，都可以使用本片語。

② **It's just like a coin having two sides**

解析 It's just like a coin having two sides意思是就像硬幣有兩

面，從另一個角度看，就是要人別只看到不好的一面。心境一轉，心情也會比較舒坦。因此，下次當看到同事在抱怨，而你又不打算吐槽而是要鼓勵他或她時，就可以使用本片語，建議他或她轉換一下看事情的角度。

③ **A crisis is a turning point**

解析 A crisis is a turning point 意思是危機就是轉機。能把危機視為一個自我挑戰，就表示心情有所轉變，所以本用法算是間接鼓勵人要正面思考。因此，下次在職場上碰到困難時，記得用這句話鼓勵自己也鼓勵別人。

E 非學不可的職場小貼示

　　Jet lag 意思是時差。若為經常出國洽公的商務人士，時差是每個人一定會碰到的狀況，所以當你有時差時，就可以用 I am still suffering from jet lag 表示。雖然人的生理時鐘也會慢慢適應，但如果在搭機過程中運用一些技巧，抵達目的時就不會感到那麼疲累。若出差的地點與出發地幾乎日夜顛倒，而你抵達的時間剛好是當地晚上的話，在航程中就不用強求自己一定要有充足睡眠。反之，如果抵達時間在白天，一下機沒多久可能馬上有行程的話，就建議在搭機時盡量睡飽。

Unit 04 Have a chip on one's shoulder 耿耿於懷

 A 辭彙文化背景介紹

　　Chip的意思是碎片，have a chip on one's shoulder直觀的意思就肩上有碎片。這個慣用語其實起源於19世紀某篇報導，文中提到當時小朋友如果要打架，會在自己的肩膀上放個碎木塊，問對方敢不敢把木塊踢下來，如果踢下就代表開打了。

　　這個片語後來也可用來形容性格，代表某人生性好鬥，心裡彷彿有出不完的怨氣，喜歡找人抬槓。更進一步看，還委婉地點出對方的行為就跟小孩子一樣幼稚。

　　若將在職場上使用此慣用語，其實不是真的要責難對方，而是要對方冷靜下來，別像小孩般無理取鬧，而是要客觀地處理事情。若抱持這樣的出發點，不論是主管對下屬，或是同事對同事，都可用此慣用語來表達欲進行理性討論的訴求。

看看辭彙怎麼用

【同事間】Between colleagues

Andy 安迪	Afternoon, Ben. We need to have a talk.	午安，班。有事要找你談談。
Ben班	What's going on, **dude**?	兄弟，怎麼了？
Andy	I have heard the rumor that you say I play tricks to get **promotion**. How come! Do you also want this title?	謠傳你說我耍手段以求升官。為什麼要這樣做！難道你也想要這個職位？
Ben	Come on, you know I won't **gossip**. <u>Don't have a chip on your shoulder.</u> Your performance in past few months is too great to ignore, so the candidate of this position tends to ruin our friendship.	拜託，你知道我從不八卦的。別覺得我再找你碴。你過去幾個月的表現好到難以忽視，所以這個職位的可能人選試圖破壞我們的友誼。
Andy	Reasonable. Sorry for doubting you.	也對。抱歉懷疑你。

Ben	Never mind, but you have to do one thing for me. Treat me to lunch today.	沒關係。但你要幫我做一件事。中午給你請。
Andy	Definitely OK. How about grabbing a sandwich in ABC Subway?	當然沒問題,去ABC潛艇堡點個三明治吃如何?
Ben	Good idea.	好主意。

【主管與屬下間】
Between the supervisor and the employee

Mark 馬克	Hey, what happened, Jill? The report you submitted to me last night has poor content.	嘿,吉兒。你是怎麼了?你昨晚寄給我的報告錯誤百出。
Jill 吉兒	I work overtime for this, but I hear no **compliment**.	我加班寫報告,但卻連句稱讚都沒有。
Mark	<u>Don't have a chip on your shoulder</u>. I don't mean to blame you. You never disappointed me in the past, so I am **curious** why such thing happened this time.	別覺得我在找碴。我並不是真的要罵你,是你過去從未讓我失望,但這次卻出包了。

Jill	I am so rude. Please accept my apology. Besides,can you give me one more hour to **revise** it?	我太魯莽了，請接受我的道歉。另外，可以再給我一小時去修改內容嗎？
Mark	Sure. I am going to attend a meeting with our supplier 30 minutes later, so you have more than one hour to finish it. I will discuss it with you when I come back this afternoon.	當然可以。我半小時後就要跟供應商開會了，所以你有不只一小時可以修改。我下午回辦公室後會跟你討論。
Jill	Get it. I will try my best to reach your expectation.	了解。我會盡全力讓您滿意。
Mark	Good. I gotta go. See you later.	很好。我該出發了，下午見。

① **dude** *n.* 夥伴們

例 Hey dude, let's finish the proposal this night.
各位夥伴們，我們今晚想辦法完成這份提案吧！

② **promotion** *n.* 晉升

例 John got promotion due to his outstanding performance when he worked as the sales representative in Spain.
約翰因為在西班牙擔任業務時的傑出表現獲得升官。

③ **gossip** *v.* 談論八卦；*n.* 八卦

例 Stop gossiping. Rumors will make the morale low.
別在八卦了，謠言會打擊公司士氣。

④ **suspect** *v.* 懷疑

例 I suspect the correctness of this financial statement.
我對這份財報的正確性感到懷疑。

⑤ **compliment** *v/n.* 稱讚

例 Jason compliments Allen on her insight analysis.
傑森對於艾倫精闢的分析表示稱讚。

⑥ **curious** *adj.* 好奇的…

例 I am curious why the sale figures suddenly drop this month.

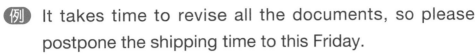

我很想知道為何這個月業績會下滑

⑦ **revise** *v.* 修正

例 It takes time to revise all the documents, so please postpone the shipping time to this Friday.

修改所有文件需要一點時間，所以請把出貨時間延到這星期五。

 D 換句話說補一補

Come on, you know I won't **gossip**.
拜託，你知道我從不八卦的。
★ Come on, you know I don't **criticize others behind**.
★ Come on, you know I don't **reveal the scandal**.
★ Come on, you know I don't **evaluate a person by mere suppositions**.

 解析時間

① **criticize others behind**

解析 criticize others behind意思就是「背後批評別人」，廣義來說，也算是在說別人的八卦。雖然說在職場上，我們針對謠言難免有知的欲望，但千萬要記得適可而止。若想有人請你對於八卦發表意見，但你不想淌渾水，就可以說I don't criticize others behind，表現出自己明人不做暗事的氣度。

② **reveal the scandal**

解析 reveal the scandal意思是「揭發醜聞」。一般來說，會成為八卦話題的事情，十件裡大概有八九件是壞事，所以道人八卦就很像是在揭發醜聞。在職場上，若得知某人的醜聞，千萬要去思考散播出去的可能後果，以免最後惹禍上身喔！

③ **evaluate a person by mere suppositions**

解析 discuss a person by mere suppositions意思是「單靠臆測來評論一個人」，相較前兩者，這種用法比較和緩些，但基本上還是沒有對於訊息來源加以查證。在職場上，我們很有可能接收到各種來源不明的消息，若這樣的消息是關於某人，而你又不想表示看法，就可以採用上述用法來表達。

Sorry for **doubting** you.
抱歉懷疑你。
★ Sorry for **not showing my faith to you**.
★ Sorry for **questioning your intent**.
★ Sorry for **making you the scapegoat**.

 解析時間

① **not showing my faith to you**

解析 not showing my faith to you意思是「對你沒有信心」，換個角度看，當我們對於某人的行為舉止，乃至於人格不表信任時，就是委婉的懷疑。在職場上，若無法相信對方，就可以使用I can't fully show my faith to you來表達懷疑。

② **questioning your intent**

〔解析〕 question one's intent意思是質疑某人的動機，換句話說，也是在表示懷疑。此一說法著重在對方為何要這樣做，將心理層面視為不信任的理由。在職場上，當你質疑對方的動機時，就可以使用此說法。發現自己錯怪別人時，也可以在前面加上I am sorry/sorry for來表達歉意。

③ **making you the scapegoat**

〔解析〕 making someone the scapegoat的原意是「讓某人背黑鍋」，換言之，就是對某人不信任，使其承受莫須有的罪名。在職場上，當我們懷疑某人，最後卻發現錯怪他時，就可以使用I am sorry for making you the scapegoat來表達歉意。

You never **disappointed** me in the past.
你過去從未讓我失望，但這次卻出包了。

★ Your performance always **meets my expectation**.
★ You always **know what I want**.
★ You always **get my point**.

 解析時間

① **meet my expectation**

〔解析〕 meet one's expectation意思是「符合某人的期待」，換個角度看，就是達成對方所預期的結果，沒有讓其感到失望。在職場上，當要稱讚對方做出自己所期待的成果時，就可以使用此用法，來表示雙方在想法上達到一致。

② **know what I want**

解析 know what I want意思是「知道我想要怎樣的⋯」，換言之，也表示出我知道對方確切的想法，在後續的處理上理當不會有太大誤差。在職場溝通上，當我們覺得對方已經弄懂我們要什麼，就可以運用此說法來表示讚揚。

③ **get my point**

解析 get my point意思是「抓到重點」，此用法與前述兩者最大的差異在於準確度的高低。前兩者比較像是抓到大方向，但get my point可能是連細節都考慮到了。在職場溝通上，當對方總能馬上理解我們的想法，就可以使用本說法來表達。

E 非學不可的職場小貼示

　　在本單同事間的對話中有出現一個叫做 dude 的單字，這個字在青少年間使用頻繁，用來表示彼此間是親近的朋友。若在職場上使用此字，千萬記得自己的角色為何。若是同事間使用，是表現出你把同事當朋友，大家可以一起努力打拼。若你是管理階層，是表現出你的親和力，把團隊裡的成員都當成朋友，而不是單純你所統轄的下屬。了解這樣的用法後，下次要找同事幫忙，或是要凝聚團隊向心力時，都可以使用 dude 一字來增加彼此的親近感。

Unit 05 See eye to eye 看法相同

A 辭彙文化背景介紹

　　眼睛是表達感受的重要器官，從眼神的變化可以得知對方的感受為何。See eye to eye原意指的眼睛與眼睛對看，當雙方眼神交換後，等同進行的一次無聲的意見交換。

　　在與人溝通時，若彼此的意見相左，在眼神上其實難以交流。相反地，若彼此意見相近，眼神交流自然就多。根據這樣的邏輯，看對眼代表思維上出現交叉點，使see eye to eye後來就衍生出「看法相同」的意思。

　　若將see eye to eye運用在職場溝通上，除表現出與對方想法一致外，還隱約表現出雙方的默契。當兩個人只透過眼神就可以知道對方想法，若為工作上的夥伴，效率必然很高。因此，下次若要稱讚與你默契良好的同事，不妨改用see eye to eye（我們看法相同。）來表達。

看看辭彙怎麼用

【同事間】Between colleagues

James
詹姆士　The proposal of the new project needs to be done by this Friday, but I still have many points to **clarify**. Do you have any good idea concerning the new promotion **campaign**?

這星期五就得完成新專案的提案報告了，但我有很多要地方得釐清，你對於新的促銷活動有任何想法嗎？

Kevin
凱文　How about the special sale of the **crossover** product? This series has been the best-seller for long.

推出聯名商品的特惠如何？這個系列的商品一直以來都很暢銷。

James　We see eye to eye on this point. According to my observation, cheap price is not always the **panacea**. Unique items sometimes are more attractive.

關於這點我們意見相同。根據我的觀察，低價策略不見得每次都奏效，商品的獨特與否有時更具吸引力。

Kevin　True. Since we are the exclusive agent of ABC Clothing in Asia, we can make good use of this strength.

沒錯。由於我們是ABC服飾在亞洲區的獨家代理，更應該要善加利用這項優勢。

James	You are right. I will list the top five of the most popular items in the chart to convince our manager to carry out this activity. Thank you so much, Kevin.	沒錯。我會把銷售前五名的產品列入圖表中，好說服經理執行此活動。凱文，非常謝謝你提供意見。
Kevin	You are welcome.	凱文：別客氣。

【主管與屬下間】
Between the supervisor and the employee

Alice 艾莉絲	Hey, Brown. This Wednesday the whole International Sales Department will have a meeting concerning the new marketing activity next year, do you have any good thought already?	嘿，布朗。本周三國貿部要針對明年度行銷活動開會，你現在有什麼好想法了嗎？
Brown 布朗	Since the performance in the US market is the most outstanding one among all, I strongly suggest that we should have more **input** in this region.	由於美國市場是我們銷售成績最好的地方，我強烈建議我們應該多投入些資源在這個區域。

Alice	<u>We see eye to eye on this point.</u>The economy has great up-downs in the past few years, so not to take the risk is a better choice.	關於這點我們意見相同。過去幾年經濟震盪劇烈，別冒險比較好。
Brown	True. Being conservative is not always bad. I suggest that we cooperate with the local distributor to gain more share next year.	沒錯。保守也不見得都是壞事。我建議明年與當地的經銷商合作，以爭取更多的市占率。
Alice	Good idea. Do you have the pocket list?	好主意。那你有口袋名單了嗎？
Brown	Yes, I have some. In terms of the coverage, B&H is the best one. However, in terms of the customer satisfaction rate, Desco enjoys good **reputation**. I will send you the chart I have integrated later.	有一些。如果單看市佔率，B&H最高。但如果換看顧客滿意度，Desco最好。我等下會把整合過的圖表寄給妳。
Alice	Great. I am so lucky to have an employee with great abilities like you.	太棒了。我很慶幸有你這樣有能力的員工。
Brown	Not to mention that. I just fulfill my duty.	別這樣說，我只是盡本份而已。

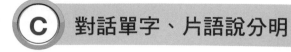

① **clarify** *v.* 釐清

例 We have to clarify which distribution channel we will use first if we want to enter this market.

若要進入此市場，需要先釐清所適用的銷售通路為何。

② **campaign** *n.* 活動

例 This promotion campaign hits the market, so we tend to hold the follow-ups next month.

這個促銷活動市場反應良好，所以我們傾向下個再舉辦後續活動。

③ **crossover** *adj.* 聯名的

例 To stimulate the purchasing, crossover items have become the main stream.

為了刺激消費，聯名商品已成主流。

④ **panacea** *n.* 萬靈丹

例 Low price is not always the panacea to the gain more market share.

低價策略不見得可以搶得更多市佔率。

⑤ **marketing** *adj.* 行銷的

例 Finding the know-how of successful marketing mode is the ultimate goal for corporates.

找出成功行銷模式的關鍵是所有公司行號的終極目標。

⑥ **input** *v.* 投入

例 To get a foot stand in the new market, you have to input certain resources.

要在新市場立足，得投入一定的資源。

⑦ **reputation** *n.* 名聲

例 Good reputation in the market takes time to accumulate, so we should be more patient.

享譽市場需要時間，所以我們要更有耐心。

D 換句話說補一補

According to my observation, cheap price is not always the **panacea.**

根據我的觀察，低價策略不見得每次都奏效。

★ According to my observation, cheap price is not always **the cure of all. .**

★ According to my observation, cheap price is not always **the solution to the problem.**

★ According to my observation, cheap price is not always **the only deciding factor.**

解析時間

① **the cure of all**

解析 the cure of all原意是「可治百病的藥」，故引申用來表示可應付各種狀況的方法。在職場上，若能找到一體適用各種事件的操作模式，無疑是一大福音，因此當有人真的提出應用廣泛的做法，或是你想稱讚對方的方法解決很多問題，都可以使用the cure of all。

② **the solution to the problem**

解析 the solution to the problem原意是「問題的答案」，換某個角度看，就像是緩解某種病症的藥物，只不過病症是發生在事情上，而不是人身上。在職場上，大家都講求效率，因此當對方找到解決困境的關鍵因子，不妨用you find the solution to the problem來表示稱讚。

③ **the only deciding factor**

解析 the only deciding factor意思是「唯一的決定因素」，換言之，就是這個因素左右了整個結果。若運用在職場溝通上，此用法多以負面的角度切入，提醒參與討論的相關人士，是否有思考不周延之處。因此，當你對於某人的想法感到疑惑，便可使用I am not that sure is this the only deciding factor.或是相似句型來給予提醒。

Since we are exclusive agent of ABC Clothing in Asia, we can **make good use of** this strength.
由於美國市場是我們銷售成績最好的地方，我強烈建議我們應該多投入些資源在這個區域。

★ Since we..., we can **optimize** this strength.
★ Since we..., we can **utilize** this strength.
★ Since we..., we can make it as our **bargaining chip**.

 解析時間

① **optimize**

解析 optimize意思是「最優化」，是科技產業經常使用的單字，故也可引申為找到最好的使用方式。在職場上，完成一件任務的方法可以很多種，但一定有某幾種是相對省時省力的，因此我們找到自家公司的優點與發揮此優點的方法時，就可以用this way can optimize...這類的句型加以表達。

② **utilize**

解析 utilize意思是「善加運用」，是設施（utility）的動詞型態。設施之所以有作用，就是有先對需求進行調查，才製作對應的器材設備。在執行業務上，找到自身優勢還不夠，如何善用更重要。因此，下次若要強調此點，便可使用utilize。

③ **bargaining chip**

解析 bargaining chip意思為「談判時的籌碼」。籌碼的概念是來自於賭博，有籌碼才能繼續玩，因此後來當上談判桌時，大家也習慣把自己所擁有的優勢或條件稱為籌碼。在職場上，

談判在所難免，了解自己有哪些籌碼，將有助於在談判過程中取得上風。例如，發現銷售通路（distribution channel）是最大優勢時，不妨這麼說Distribution channel is our bargaining chip。

I suggest that we can **cooperate with** the local distributor to gain more share next year.
我建議明年與當地的經銷商合作，以爭取更多的市占率。
★ I suggest that we can **establish partnership** with the local distributor...
★ I suggest that we can **share the market** with the local distributor...
★ I suggest that we can **form the strategic alliance** with the local distributor...

 解析時間

① **establish partnership**

　解析 establish partnership意思是「建立夥伴關係」，由於雙方會以口頭或文書的方式相互承諾，故屬於較正式的合作。在職場上，若在尋找合作夥伴的過程中，發現雙方意向已經明確，就可以用 let's establish partnership來表示高度的合作意願。

② **share the market**

　解析 share the market意思是「分享市場」，換個角度看，就是願

意與其他公司合作,不獨佔整個市場。在職場上,少一個競爭對手,多一個合作夥伴基本上利絕對多於弊。因此,在洽談合作的時候,為求談判順利,在不損及自身利益的前提下,we can share the market 會是個很好用的句子。

③ **form the strategic alliance**

解析 form the strategic alliance 意思為「成立策略聯盟」,而這樣的合作是因為某種特殊目的建立。在職場上,沒有人會願意吃虧,因此即便合作也是各取所需。因此,當權衡利益得失後,發現與該公司合作可以獲得更大利益,便可提出 maybe we can form a strategic alliance 這類的問句,提高彼此合作的機率。

 E 非學不可的職場小貼示

　　Panacea 指的是盤尼西亞這種藥物,盤尼西亞是一種抗生素,在發明之初,效用非常良好,可緩解多種病症,因此後來就引申出可以解決任何事情的萬靈丹的意思。Panacea 雖已成為職場上常見的用字,但在使用時要留意當中的些許負面意涵。因為抗生素雖然有效,但有些副作用。同樣地,再好的解決方法也可能損及部分自身利益。

Unit 06 Get on one's nerves (toes) 使人不悅

 A 辭彙文化背景介紹

　　如果直譯get on one's nerves/toes，意思就是「踩在某人的神經／腳趾上」。而神經與腳趾兩者之間又存在一個相似性，就是都很敏感。因此，各位可以想像看看，如果有東西持續壓迫到你的神經或是腳趾，那種不舒服感應該是難以忍受的。

　　由於生理的反應會影響心理的反應，當處於疼痛狀態一段時間後，心情也會跟著變差。就是依據上述的邏輯，get on one's nerve 也就產生讓人不安或反感的意涵了。

　　在職場上，難免會碰到出現天兵或是專門扯後腿的人。如果很不幸地，你剛好有這樣的同事，而你又剛好被他或她的白目行為激怒了，就可以用he/she really get on my nerves/toes來表達心中的不爽。

看看辭彙怎麼用

【同事間】Between colleagues

Henry 亨利	I can't believe Tim just told me he couldn't get her **analysis** done today. The deadline of the report is around the corner, so he really knows how to create a big trouble for everyone.	我沒辦法相信提姆跟我說他沒辦法今天就完成分析。截止日就快到了，他真會替我們找麻煩。
Teresa 泰瑞莎	The **due date** is supposed to be this Wednesday, right?	交期應該這星期三對吧？
Henry	YES! He really gets on my nerves. Now I have to make up **excuses** to convince Kyle that he can't get the outline today.	沒錯。他搞得我非常緊張。現在我得編個理由說服凱爾，跟他說今天他無法拿到報告大綱了。
Teresa	Actually I am not surprised. Tim is poor at time management, so he often **underestimates** the time needed for a task. Same thing happened last time. The report was done at the very last minute. I hate to say this, but Tim is really a troublemaker in our group.	其實我並不驚訝。提姆的時間管理能力很差，常常低估處理事情所需的時間。就像上次，他的報告也是拖到快來不及才完成。我不太想這樣說，但他真的是我們團隊中的麻煩製造機。

Henry	It seems he doesn't care about being blamed because our boss only evaluates team performance. We should teach Tim a lesson or we have to clear up his mess.	看來他似乎不怕被罵，因為老闆只針對團隊表現作評比。我們得給提姆一個教訓，不然得一直幫他收爛攤子。
Teresa	True. Maybe we can recommend him as the head of the market survey team, and then he has to make the presentation to our boss every week. I believe he will deeply understand the importance of time management after this task.	沒錯。或許我們可以推薦提姆擔任市場調查團隊的主管，那他就必需每週向老闆做簡報。我深信在做完這個案子後，提姆就會深深體會到時間管理的重要性。

【主管與屬下間】

Between the supervisor and the employee

| Jeremy
傑洛米	Mike, how's the preparation of the meeting next week?	麥可，下週會議準備得如何了？
Mike
麥克	Everything is about to be done.	一切都要準備就緒了。

Jeremy You gave me the same response three days ago, so you somehow <u>get on my nerves</u>. Does something go wrong? Solving problem **outweighs** blaming, so just tell me the truth.

你三天前也這樣跟我說，所以你搞得我有點緊張。有出狀況嗎？解決問題比責罵你們重要，所以請跟我說實話。

Mike Ok.... Since Oden forgets to inform Kelly the date of this meeting, so she might be **absent** if she can't change her schedule in time. Oden told me that he can give the final confirmation by this afternoon.

好的…。因為歐登忘記告知凱利開會的日期，所以如果凱莉無法及時更改行程的話，就會缺席本次會議。歐登告訴我說他今天下午會跟我做最後確認。

Jeremy That's all?

就只有這個問題嗎？

Mike The other thing is about **refreshments**. The GTE Food Company just informed me twenty minutes ago that they find it hard to make 100 sandwiches in time because their ovens were broken yesterday. I have contacted another bakery to prepare cupcakes.

另一個問題是關於茶點。GTE食品公司20分鐘前打給我說他們的烤箱昨天壞了，所以無法及時提供100個三明治給我們。我已經聯絡另一家麵包坊準備杯子蛋糕。

C 對話單字、片語說分明

① **analysis** *n.* 分析

例 To find the exact reason of this shutdown, the technician uses the backstage to get analyses.

為了找出當機的確切原因，技術人員使用後台系統進行分析。

② **due date** *n.* 截止日

例 The due day of this project is coming, but I still got one more report to finish.

專案的截止日快到了，可是我還有一份報告沒有寫完。

③ **excuse** *n.* 理由

例 The mistake comes from carelessness, so I have no excuse.

這個錯誤是因為我的粗心而產生，我難辭其咎。

④ **underestimate** *v.* 低估

例 Don't underestimate the power of e-media in marketing, or you will face great failure.

別低估電子傳媒在行銷上的影響力，否則你會遭遇重大挫敗。

⑤ **outweigh** *v.* 利大於弊

例 Getting the brand awareness outweighs making money when we enter this market for the first year.

在進入此市場的第一年，建立品牌知名度比賺到錢更重要。

⑥ **absent** *adj.* 缺席的

例 Sorry for being absent from your birthday. My schedule this week is too tight.

很抱歉缺席你的慶生會，本週我的行程實在太滿了。

⑦ **refreshment** *n.* 茶點

例 It's the break time of this meeting, so everyone can have some refreshments now.

現在是本次會議的休息時間，所以各位可以去享用茶點。

 D 換句話說補一補

Tim is poor at time management, so he often **underestimates** the time needed for a task.

提姆的時間管理能力很差，常常低估處理事情所需的時間。

★ Tim is poor at time management, so he often **has the wrong judgment in** the time needed for a task.

★ Tim is poor at time management, so he often **leaves inadequate time** for a task.

★ Tim is poor at time management, so he often **has no buffer time** for a task.

解析時間

① **has the wrong judgment in**

解析 has the wrong judgment in意思是「做出錯誤判斷」，如果在時間預估上出錯，其中一種情況就是低估。

② **leaves inadequate time**

解析 leaves inadequate time意思是「沒有預留充足時間」。低估所需時間也就是沒有留下足夠的時間，因此兩者在用法上可以互換。

③ **has no buffer time**

解析 has no buffer time意思是「沒有緩衝時間」。在時間掌控上，除非稍稍高估，否則基本上不存在緩衝時間，因此低估時間也等於沒有緩衝空間。所以，當我們發現自己或是同事把時間算得太緊繃或是根本低估時，就可以用we have no buffer time to...來表示。

We should teach Tim a lesson or we have to **clear up his mess**. 我們得給提姆一個教訓，不然得一直幫他收爛攤子。

★ We should teach Tim a lesson or we have to **solve the problems for him all the time**.

★ We should teach Tim a lesson or we will **get in the trouble he has made.**.

★ We should teach Tim a lesson or we have to **settle down the chaos he creates.**

解析時間

① **solve the problems for sb. all the time**

解析 solve the problems for him all the time 意思是「總是要替…解決問題」，與「幫某人收爛攤子」意思相近，只是語氣稍微委婉。因此，下次當你覺得同事老是在闖禍，但不想講地太明，就可以用 Please...., or I have to solve the problem for you all the time 來表示。

② **get in the trouble he has made**

解析 get in the trouble he has made 意思「淌他所弄出的渾水」。沒有人會沒事把麻煩攬在身上，所以在職場上，如果看到同事出包，而你想撇清時，就可以用 I don't want to get in the trouble you have made. 來表示。

③ **settle down the chaos he creates**

解析 settle down the chaos he creates 意思是「處理好他弄出的混亂場面」。在職場上，如果是只看團隊表現的公司，團隊中只要有一兩個會扯後腿的人，其他成員就得替她/他收拾殘局。所以，當你工作時真的遇到上述情況時，就可以用 I have to settle down the chaos sb. creates 來表示。

Since Oden forgets to inform Kelly the date of this meeting, so she might **be absent** if she can't change her schedule in time.

因為歐登忘記告知凱利開會的日期，所以如果凱莉無法及時更改行程的話，就會缺席本次會議。

★ Since Oden..., so she **can't show up** if she can't change her schedule in time.

★ Since Oden..., so she **would be unable to attend** if she can't change her schedule in time.

★ Since Oden..., so she **can't participate in** unless she can change her schedule in time.

 解析時間

① **can't show up**

解析 can't show up意思是「不能出席」，換句話說就是因故缺席。在職場上，若在時間上有閃失，很容易出現多個會議或是活動都選在同一時間舉行。當你選擇參加其一，就可以用I can't show up due to...這樣的句型跟其他主辦單位告知自己會缺席。

② **would be unable to attend**

解析 would be unable to attend意思是「將無法參加」。無法參加同樣也意味缺席，但此用法的would有表現出想去但去不了的無奈感，在語氣上比較有禮貌。因此，下次當我們在工作上因故無法參加某一活動時，就可以用I would be unable to attend due to...來表示。

③ **can't participate in unless...**

解析 can't participate in unless... 意思是「除非…否則無法參加」。與前面用法不同之處在於此用法強調的是如何調配出時間。因此，往後當你告知對方須更改行程才能如願參加某一活動時，就可以用 I can't participate in unless... 來表示。

 E 非學不可的職場小貼示

　　在職場上，Time management（時間管理）是一門非常重要的學問，良好的時間管理可以事半功倍，不好的時間管理會讓大家精神緊繃。時間管理的重點在於有效分配各項工作所需的時間，並且預留彈性。在本單元的換句話說單元中，所提到的 buffer time 指的就是緩衝時間。這段時間多數是用來處理突發狀況，如果一進行順利，工作如期完成，這段時間就可以讓大家喘口氣。

　　因此，不論你是員工還是主管，如果提醒別人注意時間，就可以用 watch out your time management and leave some buffer time 這類的句型來表示。

Chit-chat 閒聊

A 辭彙文化背景介紹

若要表達聊天，英文中可以使用talk、communication、chat等字，但這三個字所呈現的意涵略有差異。Talk、communication所談論的主題可能還帶有些正式性，但chat的主題就比較偏向八卦、抱怨或簡短討論等非正式話題。

而chit本身是便條（紙）的意思，便條紙通常都小小一張，主要用來簡單記事，或是將不便說出的內容文字化。因此，chit不只可以做正事，也可以傳遞八卦。

當chit加上chat，形成chit-chat這個新字時，又會產生怎樣的火花呢？這個字經常用來表達同事間在茶水間或是午休用餐時短暫的談話。對話會是抱怨某個主管或同事，或是談論某某人的八卦。但chit-chat也並非全然都用在發牢騷，主管對下屬或是同事間的簡短討論，也是用法之一。因此chit-chat是個相當常見且實用的職場用語喔！

B 看看辭彙怎麼用

【同事間】Between colleagues

Susan 蘇珊	Hey, guess who I **ran into** at the staff **cafeteria**. I met Amy!!!	嘿，猜猜我在員工餐廳遇到誰？艾咪耶！
Lucy 露西	Amy? I haven't seen her for a long time. What happened to her?	你遇到艾咪！我很久沒看到她了，她到底發生甚麼事了？
Susan	I am curious, too, so I chit-chat with her for the whole lunch time.	我也很好奇，所以我整個午餐時間都在跟她閒聊。
Lucy	Does she tell you the reason? Or she tries to **beat around the bush**?	那她有告訴你原因嗎？還是她都顧左右而言他呢？
Susan	She told me that she took a three-week business trip to settle down the troubles John made in Singapore. John promised our customer that he will receive the product this Friday, but our factory found it possible.	她說她出差三週去解決約翰在新加坡闖出的禍。約翰跟客戶保證這星期五可以收到產品，但我們工廠這邊發現根本無法如期。

Lucy	I'm not surprised. Most of John's words are like **the pie in the sky.** It looks great but you can't get it.	我不意外耶！約翰講的話大多都像是畫大餅，看的到卻吃不到。
Susan	Amy is really **outstanding** in public relation and risk management. Our boss made a wise choice. Now all the problems have been solved.	艾咪的公關跟危機管理能力真的很棒，我們的老闆做了個睿智的決定。現在所有問題都解決了。
Lucy	Indeed. Next time when I meet Amy, I should ask her how she made it.	是啊！下次我碰到艾咪，我應該請教她是如何做到的。

【主管與屬下間】

Between the supervisor and the employee

| Bob 鮑伯 | Good morning, Judy. Are you available to talk now? | 茱蒂早安，現在有空說話嗎？ |
| Judy 茱蒂 | Morning, for sure. For what topic? | 早安，當然有空。要討論什麼呢？ |

Bob	I need to <u>chit-chat with you about</u> the **latest** project. Since I'm going to brief it first to the Sales Department this afternoon, I need to re-confirm some key points with you. This is a project with great potential, and I want to make the sales team satisfied.	喔，別擔心。我只是需要和你小聊一下最新的企劃案。因為我要先讓銷售部知道我們的大綱，然後需要先和你確認你提出的一些意見。這個案子很有潛力，我想要讓銷售部滿意。
Judy	I got it. Let me prepare the slide and set the projector for a few minutes. And by the way, do you need me to grab some coffee for you?	了解。讓我準備一下投影片與開投影機。順帶一提，要幫你拿杯咖啡嗎？
Ben	Sounds good.	聽起來不錯。

C 對話單字、片語說分明

① **to run into somebody (something)** *ph.* 不期而遇/無意間發現

例 I run into the former college in the trade show in Taipei.
我在台北商展遇到前同事。

② **staff cafeteria** *n.* 員工餐廳

例 To be honest, eating our staff cafeteria is a good way to save money.
老實說，在我們員工餐廳吃飯可以省不少錢。

③ **beat around the bush** *idiom.* 拐彎抹角

例 Don't beat around the bush. We need to have a conclusion in the meeting.
別再拐彎抹角了，這個會議需要有個結論。

④ **the pie in the sky** *idiom.* 不切實際的事物

例 This project is like the pie in the sky, so I want you to modify the direction.
這個計劃太不切實際了，所以我希望你修正計畫方向。

⑤ **outstanding** *adj.* 傑出的；重要的

例 Even though you are outstanding in this field, you still need to watch out your attitude when you are green in our company.
即使你在這個領域很傑出，但當你是菜鳥時，還是要注意自己的

態度。

⑥ **latest** *adj.* 最新的；*n.* 最新的事物

例 To find the niche market, you should keep an eye on the latest trend.

為了找出利基市場，你須隨時留意最新趨勢。

⑦ **re-confirm** *v.* 再次確認

例 To make sure our customer can receive the product in time, please re-confirm the shipping date.

為確保客戶可以即時收到貨品，請再次確認出貨日期。

D 換句話說補一補

Hey, guess who I **ran into** at the staff cafeteria.

嘿，猜猜我在員工餐廳遇到誰？

★ Hey, guess who I **bumped into** at the staff cafeteria.

★ Hey, guess who I **came across** at staff cafeteria.

★ Hey, guess who I **met** at the staff cafeteria **by chance**.

 解析時間

① **bump into sb./ sth.**

解析 bump 的原意是碰撞，若以 bump into 表達巧遇，可強調相

遇時的驚訝感，因此在職場中，當我們突然遇到自己許久不見的上司、同事或客戶時，可以運用此片語表達自己出乎意料的感受，間接凸顯對方對自己的重要性。

② come across sb./ sth.

解析 across 的本意是越過或是交叉，若與 come 連用，則產生出一種意外地來到你面前的感覺。當我們在工作遇到自己覺得不太可能碰到的人時，就可以用 come across 來表現自己的驚訝感。

③ meet sb./ sth. by chance

解析 by chance 是用來表示意外地、偶然地。當放在 meet 後面做修飾語時，可以用來強調相遇的機率不高，因此碰到會覺得特別驚訝。在職場上，當彼此都業務繁忙，幾乎沒機會碰面，但卻在意料之外的場合相遇時，就可以用此片語表達自己的感受。

Amy is **outstanding** in public relation and risk management.
艾咪在公關與危機管理方面的表現真的很棒。

★ Sophia's performance in public relation and risk management **stands out** from the others.

★ Sophia **is second to none** in public relation and risk management.

★ Sophia **masters / is a master** in public relation and risk management.

解析時間

① **stand out**

解析 stand out 的原意是站出來，由於站出來的人位置會與其他人不同，後引伸出優秀的人跟其他人比較後，兩者的差異就很明顯。在職場上，若我們要誇讚別人時，不論是真心還是應酬式的稱讚，都可善加利用此片語，以凸顯出被你稱讚的人到底有多傑出。

② **second to none**

解析 second to none意思指的是不輸給任何人，換句話說，就是指某人／事物是最好的。若把此片語運用在職場的稱讚語中，還可表達出被稱讚的當事人可能因為謙虛而不敢當，但我卻覺得你如果說自己是第二，沒人會是第一的意思，是種迂迴但高竿的恭維方式。

③ **master / master in**

解析 master若當名詞用，指的是碩士。若當動詞用，是表示精通某事。在職場上，當我們要選擇以master稱讚對方時，除了肯定對方的能力外，還間接表達出對方所使用的方式實屬正規，非靠旁門左道獲得成功。

I want to **make** the sales team **satisfied**.

我想要讓銷售部滿意。

★ I want to **meet** the sales team's **expectation**.

★ I want to makethe sales team **turn thumbs up**.

★ I **want** the sales team **to be content**.

 解析時間

① **meet one's expectation**

解析 meet one's expectation 指的是符合某人的期待，換個角度看，也代表能讓對方滿意。在職場上，有時候做好但方向不對，等於做錯，因此記得要先弄懂對方的需求，才能對症下藥。

② **turn thumbs up**

解析 若思考片語 turn thumbs up 為何使用 thumbs 而不是 thumb，就會發現用複數更可代表感到滿意之意。在職場上，當我們舉出一隻大拇指時，代表此想法很不錯，但可能還找的到一些修正空間，當舉出雙手的大拇指時，就代表幾乎無可挑剔。因此未來如果非常肯定對方的想法，不妨使用 turn thumbs up。

③ **to be content**

解析 content 若當名詞用，有「內容」的意思。因此轉作動詞時，做「滿意」用。我們之所以會覺得滿意，一定是可以接受其內容，因此在職場上，不論是要表達自己感到滿意，或是希望對方滿意，都可以使用 content 一字。

E 非學不可的職場小貼示

　　對話中的grab some coffee其實是一個常見用法。在討論公事時，許多人習慣手邊有杯咖啡，邊喝邊進行意見交換。由於grab表現出快速或是順道拿取的意思，也符合多數公司所要求的高效率形象。因此下次問主管或同事是否需要喝杯咖啡或是拿個東西，不妨改用grab當動詞，例如Please grab some coffee for me when go downstairs，意思就是「等等你下樓的時候，順邊幫我買杯咖啡好嗎？」。

Unit 08 Split hairs 鑽牛角尖

 辭彙文化背景介紹

Split 意思是「劈開」，我們直覺會想到就是劈柴（split the wood）這類的情況。學習動作要領後，順利把柴劈開並不困難，但如果今天把劈開的物體換成頭髮，難度是不是就非常高了！

另外，從功用的層面來看，分開頭髮的意義實在不大，所以spilt hair就可引申為形容某人吹毛求疵，會把心力花費在不重要的事情上，又或是硬要把事情分析到非常細微，鑽牛角尖。

在職場溝通上，相信大家都很害怕碰到這種人。這種性格的人除了愛堅持己見外，最糟的是會拖累討論進度，或是弄偏討論方向。所以，下次開會或是與同事討論時，若發現上述情況，記得用 Don't split hair. Let's... 這樣的句型來使溝通更加順暢。

B 看看辭彙怎麼用

【同事間】Between colleagues

Ken 肯	How do you feel about the design of the new poster for the summer sale?	你覺得夏季特賣海報的設計如何？
Jessica 潔西卡	The **alphabetical order** of my name is not right. I should come before Judy.	我名字的字母排列順序不對，我應該要排在茱蒂前面。
Ken	Ok, that is a mistake. But can you review it in a bigger picture! We need to check it **comprehensively**. I think the upper part uses too many dark colors, so this poster is not that eye-catching if people see it from distance.	嗯，這確實是個錯誤，但可以請你更宏觀一點嘛！我們需要全面性的檢視。我覺得海報的上半部用了太多深色，遠看不太吸引人。
Jessica	What I just said is very important because a good poster needs to be perfect.	我剛說的很重要啊！因為海報不能有錯誤。
Ken	Come on! Don't split hairs. Please give me some **practical** suggestions.	你行行好，別在那鑽牛角尖。給點有建設性的意見。

Jessica	Alright, I feel the background in the central part makes it hard for me to read the instruction. The idea itself is **awesome**, but the color shall be lighter.	好啦！我覺得中間背景的部分，讓我很難好好閱讀上面的文字。設計本身很棒，但顏色應該淡一點。
Ken	Now we have found two parts worthy of discussion. I will inform Leo of a meeting with us to revise the design tomorrow. Thank you, Jessica.	現在我們找出兩個值得討論的地方了。我會找里歐明天跟我們一同修正設計。潔西卡，感謝你的意見。
Jessica	You are welcome.	別客氣。

【主管與屬下間】
Between the supervisor and the employee

Frank 法蘭克	Have you checked the report for the meeting tomorrow, Helen?	海倫，明天開會要用的報告都檢查好了嗎？
Helen 海倫	I am checking now. Please give me one more working hour.	我正在檢查。再給我一個小時。
Frank	Let's check together. Please connect your notebook with the projector.	一起檢查好了。請把筆電連接投影機。

Helen	OK. Give me few minutes.	好的，請等我幾分鐘
	(Helen sets up the machine and opens the file)	（海倫架好機器並打開檔案）
Frank	Don't you find any mistakes? I found that the notes shall be added under the **formula**; otherwise, our customer will feel confused. And I think we shall use red color to highlight the key points.	你有發現任何錯誤嗎？我發現公式底下應該要加註，不然客戶會很困惑。另外，我覺得應該用紅色標示重點。
Helen	The **diagram** is not in the central part. It is in one space more to the left.	圖表沒有置中，往左偏了一個空格。
Frank	It is not that important. One click can solve this problem. <u>Please do not split hairs.</u>	這沒那麼重要。按一下置中功能就好了。別那麼鑽牛角尖。
Helen	I find a typo in the chapter 3. The last word in line three should be **departure** rather than boarding.	我發現第三張有打錯字。第三行的最後一個字應該是離開而不是裝船。
Frank	Good.	做得好。

C 對話單字、片語說分明

① **alphabetical** *adj.* 字母的

例 It will be easy for you to check who is absent from the meeting if attendees on the list are arranged by their alphabetical order.

如果你按照字母排序與會者名單的話，就很容易知道誰缺席了。

② **comprehensively** *adv.* 全面地

例 Since we can't find the reason of the unexpected shutdown of the machine, the examination needs to be made comprehensively.

由於找不到突然當機的原因，所以要進行全免檢修。

③ **practical** *adj.* 實際的

例 What we need is a practical suggestion, so please be more serious.

我們需要實際的建議，所以請不要開玩笑。

④ **awesome** *adj.* 優秀的

例 The performance of the machine is awesome, so I think it will hit the market soon.

新機器的效能很棒，所以我相信它很快就可以席捲整個市場。

⑤ **formula** *n.* 公式

例 It seems that we have to revise one parameter in

this formula, or we will get the wrong outcome in the financial statement.

看來我們需要修正公式裡的其中一個參數，否則整份財報的計算結果會是錯的。

⑥ **diagram** *n.* 圖表

例 From the trend in this diagram, we can tell that the sales figure sharply drop in the quarter 3.

從此圖表的趨勢看來，第三季的銷售數字大幅下滑。

⑦ **departure** *n.* 離開

例 Please double check the departure time of truck, or you will miss the time for boarding.

請再次注意卡車的時間，否則會趕不上裝船時間。

D 換句話說補一補

I think the upper part uses too many dark colors, so this poster is not that **eye-catching** if people see it from distance.

我覺得海報的上半部用了太多深色，遠看不太吸引人。

★ I think upper part use too many dark colors, so this poster can't **hit people between their eyes** if people see it from distance.

★ I think the upper part uses too many dark colors, so this poster is not that **incomparable** if people see it from distance.

★ I think the upper part uses too many dark colors, so this poster can't **draw people's attention** if they see it from distance.

 解析時間

① **hit people between their eyes**

解析 hit people between their eyes意思是「令人印象深刻」。這個用法是源自於當物體從雙眼中間襲來,人體會馬上做出反應。而由於這樣的反應往往很激烈,後來就衍生出印象深刻的意涵。在職場上,如果覺得對方提出的意見很能吸引目光,不妨使用hit people between their eye來表達自己的想法。

② **incomparable**

解析 incomparable意思是「無與倫比的」。若單看字首in與comparable,可能會感覺此負面字,但事實上卻是正面意涵(沒人比得上,所以是最好)。在職場上,若要以此字稱讚對方,最好思考一下適切性,因為該字語意強度較高,使用不當會讓人感覺是在諂媚。

③ **draw one's attention**

解析 draw one's attention意思「吸引某人注意」,換個角度看,就代表能夠使人停下腳步多看幾眼。在職場上,若以此稱讚對方的設計或是構想,代表這樣的設計或構想成功抓到目標族群

的喜好，使其注意力馬上停留於此，因此，下次覺得對方抓到
你的胃口時，不妨以此用法給予肯定。

Now we have found two parts **worthy of discussion.**
現在我們找出兩個值得討論的地方了。

★ Now we have found two parts that still **have the room for modification**

★ Now we have found two parts that **need some opinion exchange.**

★ Now we have found two parts **that haven't reached the consensus.**

 解析時間

① **have the room for modification**

解析 have the room for modification意思是「尚有修正空
間」，換言之，就是還需要討論。在職場溝通上，若無法完全
同意對方看法，又怕措辭太強烈，不妨使用have the room
for modification 委婉地表達自己的立場。

② **need some opinion exchange**

解析 need some opinion exchange意思是「需要意見交換」，
換言之，同樣是需要進一步討論。在職場溝通上，若雙方立場
相左且有些僵持不下時，不妨使用we need some opinion
exchange來緩和氣氛，讓溝通可以繼續進行。

③ **haven't reached the consensus**

解析 haven't reached the consensus意思為「尚未達成共識」，從另一個角度看，同樣代表需要更多討論。在職場溝通上，只要存有模糊空間，未來執行上就容易有爭議，因此未來如果發現還有細節沒確定，就可以用haven't reached consensus來表示。

Otherwise our customer will feel **confused.**

★ Otherwise our customer will **have the chance to misunderstand.**

★ Otherwise our customer **may make wrong judgment.**

★ Otherwise our customer will **have doubts.**

 解析時間

① **have the chance to misunderstand**

解析 have the chance to misunderstand意思是「有可能會誤解」，換個角度看，就是因為心中有疑惑，而產生錯誤的判斷或解讀。在職場上，若要提醒大家不要因溝通誤差而造成損失，就可使用we need make the argument have no chance to be misunderstood或是類似句型加以告知。

② **make wrong judgment**

解析 make wrong judgment意思是「做出錯誤判斷」，從發生原因的角度看，同樣是源自於對於事物有疑惑。在職場上，一個錯誤判斷可使後續工作全盤皆錯。因此，若要提醒大家

讓對方判斷錯誤的嚴重性所在，就可使用 we should avoid making people make wrong judgment 這類句型做表示。

③ have doubts

解析 have doubts 意思「有疑惑」，換個角度切入，也是源自於資訊有模糊空間。從職場溝通的角度看，沒有疑惑就能加速達成共識，讓事情進行順利。因此，下次在討論過程中若覺得有疑惑，I have some doubts 就會是很好用的句子。若沒有疑惑，想表示贊成，則可使用 I have no doubts。

 E 非學不可的職場小貼示

　　Alphabetical order 指的是字母排序，乍看之下這個順序似乎沒很重要，但事實上它可以幫我們省去很多職場上所會遭遇麻煩。在各種文宣品或是電子訊息中，通常有一部分會是關於參與單位與參與人士。其實有不少人會在意當中的順序，在沒有誰主誰從的前提下，若將某一人或單位排在前頭，另一個單位可能就會感到不悅。若要避免得罪任何人，採用字母排序是非常好的方法。因為是採用客觀依據，字母排序在前，就出現在名單的前段，反之，就排在後段，大家也就沒有爭議的空間。

Part 2
【內勤】辦公室會議篇

Unit 09　Cross one's mind 突然想到

 A 辭彙文化背景介紹

Cross有「穿過」的意思，因此過馬路可以用cross the road表示。由於馬路是具象的事物，能夠穿越聽起來似乎理所當然。但如果要穿越的是抽象的概念，乍聽之下可能會讓人一頭霧水。

直譯Cross one's mind，意思是穿過某人的想法。我們可以想像看看，如果有東西突然穿過，當下的反應肯定是最直接的，之後要刻意模仿可能還模仿不來。所以，根據這樣的邏輯，cross one' mind後來就引申出靈光乍現、驚鴻一瞥的意涵。

在職場上，好的想法不見得都是經過縝密思考得來，突然出現的靈感有時彷彿神來一筆。因此，在開會時，做為下屬，如果突然有好的想法，不妨用It crossed my mind that請大家暫停一下，聽聽自己的想法。若你是上司，也可用Raise your hand if any ideas cross your mind之類的句型鼓勵大家發言。

看看辭彙怎麼用

【同事間】**Between colleagues**

Paul
保羅

Everybody, we have to outline the **prototype** of our new logo in this meeting, so please feel free to express your ideas.

各位，我們必須在本次會議中勾勒出新商標的雛型，所以請大家暢所欲言。

Lucas
盧卡斯

How about the **abbreviation** of our company's name BUGA with the shadow beneath the **letters**?

用公司名稱的縮寫 BUGA，然後加上字母的陰影如何？

Paul

It is feasible, but I think this design is somehow not so impressive. Adding some image somewhere could be a direction.

這是可行的，但我總覺得這樣的設計很難讓人印象深刻，在文字的某處加上圖像會是個可以繼續討論的方向。

Lucas

Your words inspire me. <u>Now I have an idea crossing my mind.</u> We can keep the spirit of the design, but change the form a little bit. The full name of our company will be written in a cycle as a frame, and then we put a torch in the middle.

你的話啟發了我。現在我突然有個想法。剛所提到的設計精髓可以保留，但在形式上做些改變。公司的全銜會以一個圓圈的方式書寫做為外框，然後中間放上火炬。

	A torch is not only a **necessity** for campers, but also a symbol of taking the lead in this industry. With the two meanings combined, this design can perfectly match our brand image.	火炬除了是露營人士的必需品外，也是在業界執牛耳的象徵。結合這兩種意涵後，這個設計完全符合本公司形象。
Paul	Wonderful. This is a not prototype at all because it is mature enough to be carried out immediately.	太棒了。這根本不叫雛型，因為這設計已經成熟到可直接執行了。
Lucas	Don't mention that. If you like this idea, let's discuss the details like the color, size, and so on.	別這麼說，如果你喜歡這個想法，接下來就繼續討論顏色、尺寸等細節。

【主管與屬下間】

Between the supervisor and the employee

Sean 尚恩	The topic of the meeting today is about the sales figure.	今天會議的主題是關於銷售數字。

Strange to say, our performance in Paradise Shopping mall is worse than that of our main **competitor** ABC Clothing even we have held a special sale for one week. Please speak out if you find any clue.

說也奇怪，即使已經舉行一周特賣，我們在天堂購物中心的業績還是比ABC服飾差。各位如果有找出線索，請盡量發表看法。

Bruce
布魯斯

Both brands target the middle class, so price wouldn't be the deciding factor. Could it have something to do with advertising?

我們兩個品牌都主攻中產階級，所以價格不會是決定性因素。那會不會跟廣告有關係呢？

Sean

A very interesting argument. What's wrong with our advertisement in your opinion?

很有趣的論點。那你認為廣告哪邊有問題呢？

Bruce

What you just said reminds me to make a **comparison**. Here is an idea crossing my mind. Now let's take a look of the ads. The one on the left is ours, while the right one is ABC's. It seems ABC copies our design because the layout is 80% similar. Some consumers are cheated.

你的話提醒我應該做比較。我現在腦中有個想法，讓我們直接看看兩間公司的廣告。左手邊的是我們的，右手邊的是ABC的。看起來ABC抄襲我們的設計，這個架構有百分之八十相似。有些顧客被騙了。

Sean	Good job. We need to re-design the ad and take some **legal** action if needed.	做的好。我們需要重新設計廣告，以及在必要情況下採取法律行動。
Bruce	I will call Tom to prepare the documents.	我會聯絡湯姆準備文件。
Sean	Since we find the reason, let's wrap it up here.	既然找到原因了，會就開到這邊吧！

 對話單字、片語說分明

① **prototype** *n.* 雛型

例 This is just the prototype, and you can receive the finished product one week later.

這只是雛型，一週後你就能收到完成品。

② **abbreviation** *n.* 縮寫

例 CEO is the abbreviation of chief executive officer.

CEO是 chief executive officer（首席執行官）的縮寫。

③ **letters** *n.* 字母

例 To keep the layout of the banner neat, only 15 to 20 letters should be used.

為保持標語的版面精簡，字母最多只能放15到20個字母。

④ **necessity** *n.* 必需品

例 To gain more shares in the market, e-commerce is a necessity.

若要搶得更多市佔，電子商務勢在必行。

⑤ **competitor** *n.* 競爭者

例 PAA is our main competitor in camping equipment, so we have to create product differentiation.

PAA是我們在露營用品上的最大競爭對手，所以需要創造產品差異性。

⑥ **comparison** *n.* 比較

例 If we make a comparison between the product of top brand and ours, creativity is the aspect we have the room to improve the most.

如果比較頂尖品牌與我們公司的產品，創意是我們最需要努力的部分。

⑦ **legal** *adj.* 法律的

例 We will take a legal action if you refuse to fulfill your obligation listed in the contract.

如果您不履行合約中所載明之義務，我們會採取法律行動。

D 換句話說補一補

A torch is not only a **necessity** for campers, but also a symbol of a power

火炬除了是露營人士的必需品外，也是在業界執牛耳的象徵。

★ A torch is not only **a tool campers can't do without**, but also a symbol of a power.

★ A torch is not only **a must-bring** for campers, but also a symbol of a power.

★ A torch is not only **a sharp weapon** for campers, but also a symbol of a power.

 解析時間

① **a tool somebody can't do without**

解析 a tool somebody can do without 意思是「某人所不可或缺的工具」，換句話說，就是一定要有這項工具。因此在職場上，不論是要提醒或是請教對方何種工具或設備最好用，都可以採用 what is the tool someone can't do without 來表示。

② **a must-bring**

解析 a must-bring 意思是「必帶品」，換句話說，就是沒帶到會產生很多麻煩。在職場上，有時前輩會提醒後輩在那些場合應該要準備那些器材，所以當我們請教前輩時，不妨使用 what is the must-bring if I... 這類的句型，請前輩指點迷津。

③ **a sharp weapon**

> **解析**　a sharp weapon意思是「鋒利的武器」，乍看之下好像工具一點關係都沒有，但若從武器的功用面來看，鋒利的武器功用就很廣，因此也可引伸用來指稱好用的事物。在職場上，凡事講求快狠準，因此當你覺得對方提出的方法很能切中要點，就可以用sharp weapon稱呼之。

Part 2 【內勤】辦公室會議篇

Both brands **target** the middle class, so price wouldn't be the deciding factor.

我們兩個品牌都主攻中產階級，所以價格不會是決定性因素。

★ The middle class is **the target customer of** the two brands, so price wouldn't be the deciding factor.

★ The middle class **has the greatest potential to consume**, so price wouldn't be the deciding factor.

★ Both of two brands **share the same consumer segmentation** in the middle class, so price wouldn't be the deciding factor.

 解析時間

① **the target customer of**

> **解析**　the target customer of...意思是「…的主要客群」，換言之，就是設定最有可能會購買該商品的族群。在銷售產品上，市場區分十分重要，商品再好，設定錯客群，就可能滯銷。因此，當你要表示某個族群是你商品所設定的消費主力，就可以說...is the target customer of our product。

② **has the greatest potential to consume**

解析 has the greatest potential to consume意思是「最有消費的可能性」，換言之，就是公司最應設定的消費族群。在開會時，若手邊有相關數據或圖表，就可用...has the greatest potential to consume according to來說明自己分析後所得出之結果。

③ **share the same consumer segmentation**

解析 share the same consumer segmentation意思是「有相同的市場區格」，換言之，就是主力客群相同。在開會分析客群時，若發現與競爭對手的主力客群相仿，就可以說We share the same consumer segmentation with....。

What you just said reminds me to make a **comparison.**
你的話提醒我應該做比較。

★ What you just said reminds me to **find the differences.**
★ What you just said reminds me **to search for the contrasting parts.**
★ What you just said reminds me to **check the similarity.**

 解析時間

① **find the differences**

解析 find the differencesto意思是「找出差異處」，換個角度看，也是在做比較。開會的目的之一就是找出事情的差異點，因此當我們發現不同處時，就可以使用這種表達。

② **search for the contrasting parts**

解析 search for the contrasting parts意思是「尋找對比之處」，屬於有針對性的比較。在開會過程中，假使有需要找出在本質上相反的概念或事物來比較，就可以用I am searching for the contrasting parts...這樣的句子來表示。

③ **check the similarity**

解析 check the similarity意思是「檢查相似性」，在面向上與前種用法剛好相反，但也是在做比較。在開會過程中，若一時無法釐清差異，不妨改從相似性切入，例如let's check the similarity，再從相似中尋找新的比較點。

E 非學不可的職場小貼示

　　Abbreviation意思是縮寫，採用縮寫通常是各個單字的首字母，例如A&F就是知名美國品牌Abercrombie & Fitch的縮寫。另外，有些縮寫是截取數個單字中的某一部分加以組合，例如知名運動品牌Adidas是採用創辦人Adolf AdiDassler姓名中的Adi加上das。縮寫看起來十分簡單，但事實上包含極大的學問，巧妙的縮寫可創造無限商機。在商場上，縮寫能讓消費者有記憶點，購買的機率就能提高不少。

Unit 10 All hands on deck 大家一起動手幫忙；船長要求所有船員幫忙

 A 辭彙文化背景介紹

　　如果照字面翻譯 all hands on deck，意思就是「所有手在甲板上」。這樣的翻法相信沒人看得懂到底要表達什麼，所以接下來讓我們用逐步拆解的方式，找出它真正的意涵。

　　由於船才有甲板，所以此用法就跟航海有關。一般來說，各個船員都各司其職，船長不會隨便調動位置。但如果遭遇特殊情況，船長就有可能召集所有船員，請大家到甲板上共同處理，all hands on deck 指的就是上述的情況。也因為這層召集的含意，後來此用法就引申為「請大家幫忙」的意思。

　　在職場上，一定有機會碰到需要協助的情況。若是請同事幫忙，講出 all hands on deck，就有點像是在考驗自己的人緣好不好，若大家願意幫忙，代表平常做人還算成功。若你是主管，講出 all hands on deck，就有點像是檢視同仁對你的愛戴程度，因為主管要下屬做事理所當然，但從做的態度就可以看出下屬是心悅誠服還是心不甘情不願。

B 看看辭彙怎麼用

【同事間】Between colleagues

Ada 艾達	Hey guys, let's have a brief meeting. Now I have a good news and a bad news. Which one do you want to know first?	各位，讓我們開會一下，我現在手邊有一個好消息跟一個壞消息，想先聽哪個？
Parker 帕克	The bad one.	壞消息好了。
Ada	I get an unexpected order of 1000 **chips** from NKA Industry.	我接到NKA工業1千張晶片的訂單。
Parker	It sounds great. How come you say you have a bad news?	這聽起很好啊！怎麼會說是壞消息呢？
Ada	Why we can get this order is MAA failed to meet their **requirement** last week, so we only have one week left to produce or to get the chip they need. Please all hands on deck. We have to find the way to ship the product in time.	為什麼拿的到這張訂單是因為MAA上週無法達到NKA的要求，所以我們也只剩下一週可以生產或是取得NKA所需要的晶片。請大家幫幫忙，我們得找到方法準時出貨。

Parker	Considering the transportation time, we only have six days left. Since the mass **production** per day is 100 pieces, we still have 400 pieces left that need to be produced. **Dispatching** the inventory will be a good option. Give me few seconds to check the system.	如果把交通時間也考慮進去，我們只剩下6天。一天的最大產量是100張，所以我們還少400張。調度存貨會是好方法。給我點時間去系統查詢。
Ada	OK. Hope we have adequate goods to sell.	好的，希望有足夠的貨品可供出售。
Parker	Good news to us. The data indicate we have 450 pieces left in stock. You can get off your chest.	跟你說個好消息，系統資訊顯示尚有450張庫存，你可以放心了。
Ada	True. Now I can ask the manufacturing department to produce and call Emily to check the goods in the warehouse.	沒錯，我現在可以先請製造部開始生產，然後聯絡艾蜜莉逐步清點在倉庫裡晶片。

【主管與屬下間】

Between the supervisor and the employee

Davis 戴維斯	Everybody, time for meeting. Since JCZ wants to change the layout and adds searching functions to the system with the same budget, I need to get the **feedback** concerning this request from engineers. Please all hands on deck.	各位來開會了！因為 JCZ 想在費用不變的前提下更改架構，並在系統中增加搜尋功能，所以我需要各位工程師針對此點給我回應。請大家幫幫忙。
Miller 米勒	To add the searching function is an easy task, but to change in layout is much more complicated. We need to charge more if the range of adjustment is great.	增加搜尋功能很簡單，但更改架構就複雜多了。如果更動的幅度很大，就應該額外收費。
Luis 路易斯	What's more, the deadline shall be **extended** if we find re-coding is necessary. The working **burden** is heavy for a comprehensive change like that.	此外，如果有重新編碼的必要，截止日也應該往後延。像這種全面性的修改，其工作負擔是很重的。

Part 2

【內勤】辦公室會議篇

Miller	What we just said is the general direction.Please ask them to send specific needs to my e-mail address, and I will provide the new quotation after the professional evaluation with my team.	我們剛剛所提的只是大略的方向，還是要請他們把確切的需求透過電子郵件寄給我。在與我的團隊進行專業評估後，再給JCZ新報價。
Luis	What if they need a face-to-face discussion, I am available this Friday afternoon.	如果他們需要面對面討論的話，我這星期五下午有空。
Davis	I got it. I will integrate what you two just said and sent a formal e-mail to Mr. Lu. Thank you, Miller and Luis.	我了解了。我會整合你們的回覆，並寄一封正式的電子郵件給盧經理。謝謝，米勒跟路易斯。

Ⓒ 對話單字、片語說分明

① **chip** *n.* 晶片

例 The profit of a chip now is much lower than you think
現在晶片的利潤遠比你想的還低。

② **requirement** *n.* 要求

例 To meet this customer's requirement, we have to work

overtime tonight.

為符合此客戶的要求，今晚得加班了。

③ **production** *n.* 生產

例 The cost of each machine can be lower if the production reaches economies of scale.

如果生產達到規模經濟，每台機器的成本就會下降

④ **dispatch** *v.* 調度

例 What if you need more manpower, I can dispatch one team to you.

如果你需要更多人力的話，我可以調動一個團隊給你。

⑤ **feedback** *n.* 回饋

例 The feedback from customer is the source for us to improve.

顧客的回饋是我們進步的泉源。

⑥ **extend** *v.* 延長

例 The warranty of our products will be extended to 2 years from January this year.

本公司產品保固從今年一月起延長為2年。

⑦ **burden** *n.* 負擔

例 The wrong judgment we have made in Thailand creates heavy financial burden in Q3.

在泰國的錯誤判斷使我們第三季出現嚴重的財務負擔。

D 換句話說補一補

Dispatching the **inventory** will be a good option.
調度存貨會是好方法。

★ Dispatching **the goods stored in the warehouse** will be a good option.
★ Dispatching **the product in stock** will be a good option.
★ Dispatching **the spare product** will be a good option.

 解析時間

① **the goods stored in the warehouse**

解析 the goods stored in the warehouse意思是「存放在倉庫的貨品」。一般來說，存貨才會放倉庫。因此，若會議中討論到關於存貨的問題，也可以用此用法來替換。

② **the product in stock**

解析 the product in stock意思是「處於庫存狀態的貨品」，換句話說，這些貨品就是存貨。與上述用法不同之處，本用法著重貨品的狀態，前者則著重存放地點。因此，下次在會議過程中，針對強調的重點的不同，使用對應的說法表示「存貨」。

③ **the spare product**

解析 the spare product意思是「預備的產品」，也就是我們常聽到的備品。從目的來看，或許備品比較偏向公司自用，但廣義來說，也是先生產好來存放的，因此也算是存貨的一種。因

此，在開會中若討論到存貨問題，the spare product 也是你可以運用的一環。

You can get off your chest.
你可以放心了。
★ You can **free from worries**.
★ A weight has been lifted from your shoulder.
★ It is a great relief to you.

 解析時間

① **free from worries**

解析　free from worries 意思是「不用煩惱」。人有壓力就可能產生煩惱，因此「免於煩惱」也算是表達「不用擔心」的替代用法之一。因此，下次如果在開會時順利找到解決難題的方法，不妨使用 I /you can free from worries 來表達那種鬆一口氣的感覺。

② **A weight has been lifted from your shoulder**

解析　A weight has been lifted from your shoulder 意思是「如釋重負」，與 get off your chest 意思相近。兩者差異在於比喻的身體部位不同。本用法是把重物從肩膀放下，另一個則是胸口。理解兩種用法後，下次開會要表達終於放心時，就有好幾種選擇了。

③ **It is a great relief to you**

解析 It is a great relief to you意思是「對你而言是一大放鬆」，從另一個角度看，就是麻煩終於解決了。與前述用法不同的是，本用法沒用使用比喻，而是直接表達情緒。因此，下次在開會中討論出解決難題的方案時，不妨用It is a great relief to you/me來表達。

What's more, the deadline shall **be extended**, if we find re-coding is necessary.
如果有重新編碼的必要，截止日也應該往後延。

★ What's more, the deadline shall **have the room for negotiation** if we find re-coding is necessary.

★ What's more, the deadline shall **be adjusted** if we find re-coding is necessary.

★ What's more, the deadline shall be **flexible**if we find re-coding is necessary.

 解析時間

① **have the room for negotiation**

解析 have the room for negotiation意思是「有協商的空間」，換言之，就是沒有硬性規定。當截止日需要協商，通常是需要延後，極少數情況會是提前，因此，下次開會時若發現工作因為某些突發因素無法如期完成，需要延長工作時間時，就可以說the deadline has the room for negotiation if...來表示。

② **be adjusted**

解析 be adjusted意思是「需要調整」，是比較委婉的用法。與前述的概念相同，需要調整到期日，幾乎都是要延後，因此下次在開會過程中若想表達延後截止日的需求，就可以用 I think the deadline shall be adjust if... 這類句型來表達。

③ **flexible**

解析 flexible意思是「有彈性的」，可以用來形容時程有調整的空間。從廣義的角度看，截止日延展就代表此期限有彈性的，因此，開會時若要爭取這樣空間，就可用 the deadline shall be flexible if... 的句型來表達。

E 非學不可的職場小貼示

　　乍看對話中提到quotation一字，可能會誤以為是在講引用某種文獻，但在貿易領域中，此字指的是報價。買賣雙方會透過報價來探知對方底限大約在哪，因此報價其實一門非常大的學問。當我方接獲報價，若對此不滿意，建議直接求對方重新報價，而不要選擇還價。當中原因在於若我方還價金額高於對方最低讓步空間，其實就是一種損失。而當角色互換作為報價方時，則要盡量避免對方一直殺價，以保有充足的利潤。

Unit 11 Break the back of...
突破難關

A 辭彙文化背景介紹

　　若從字面看 break the back of... 意思是「折斷⋯⋯的背」。那背斷了會產生什麼影響，就讓我們從人的身體構造來抽絲剝繭。

　　在你我的背上，有著支撐整個身體的脊椎，萬一脊椎斷了，我們也就癱瘓無法自由行動了。因此 back 一字除了描述身體部位外，也就衍生出「主幹」的意涵。根據這樣的邏輯繼續推演，如果事情的主幹被折斷，剩下的部分就非常容易處理了。因此最後就可以推敲出 break the back of sth 意思是「是突破⋯⋯的難關」。

　　理解此用法後，往後在工作上如果成功地解決一些難題，即便還有一些細節尚待完成，如果是自己獨立處理的業務，記得用 I have broken the back of... 來勉勵自己，如果是團隊任務，也別忘了用 we have broken the back of... 來激勵團隊士氣。

B 看看辭彙怎麼用

【同事間】Between colleagues

Robert
羅伯特

Next Monday we will have a presentation concerning the progress of the software **development**, how's the part you are responsible for?

下星期我們要針對軟體開發進度做簡報，你負責的那個部分進度到哪邊了？

Downey
道尼

I have broken the back of the automatic bug detecting. Though it takes me more than one week, but now I can be proud of my **achievement**. Now it functions well, so what I need to do in the next few days is to double-check and ensure everything goes smooth in the meeting.

我已經克服自動偵錯的難關了。雖然這花掉我超過整整一星期，但現在我對我的成果感到驕傲。此功能目前都很正常，所以接下來幾天我要做的就是檢查再檢查，以確保開會時一切順暢。

Robert

Lucky you. My calculation part still has some room to improve. Although the outcomes never go wrong, the time consumed is a lot. **Simplifying** the coding is the option I should try.

你運氣真好。我的計算部分還有改善空間。雖然計算結果都是對的，但花掉的時間太多。簡化編碼是個我該去嘗試的選項。

Part 2

【內勤】辦公室會議篇

Downey	Right. Living in the Information Age, most consumers can't bear waiting too long for the answer or outcome they need.	沒錯。生在資訊世代，多數的消費者沒有耐心花太多時間等他們需要的答案或結果。
Robert	I agree. What I will do later is to modify one **instruction** in data accessing, and I hope such changes can enhance the efficiency.	這點我同意，所以等下我要修改獲取資料的指令，希望這可以成功提高效率。
Downey	Good luck man, let's go to work now. See you later in lunch time.	祝你好運。讓我們開始工作了，午餐見。

【主管與屬下間】
Between the supervisor and the employee

	(In a meeting)	（會議中）
Adam 亞當	Our new smartphone is scheduled to release in Q2 next year, so today I gather you all to have a meeting. Wendy, how is the battery part?	我們的新款智慧型手機預計於明年第二季上市，所以今天集合各位開會。溫蒂，手機電池目前狀況如何？

Wendy 溫蒂	Since a smartphone has become a **necessity** in our daily life, the volume of the battery matters a lot. <u>Holding this faith, the R&D team has broken the back of the storage limitation and developed a high efficiency battery</u>. Traditionally, the volume is directly proportional to thickness. Thicker battery has more room to store the power, but it **inevitably** makes the phone become thicker.	由於智慧型手機已經成為生活必需品，電池的容量大不大就很重要。秉持這樣的信念，我們的研發團隊已經成功突破儲存限制，開發出一款高效能手機電池。就現況來看，電池容量與厚度成正比。越厚的電池有越多電力儲存空間，但也無可避免的使整個手機厚度增加。
Joey 喬伊	True. Just because all the other competitors face such problem, our new phone will definitely hit the market. The thickness is the amazing 4mm, but its battery volume is enough for a two-day usage if the user just surfs the webs, answers, and makes phone calls.	正因為所有其他競爭者都面臨此問題，公司要推出的新手機絕對轟動市場。因為厚度才4釐米，但使用者只拿它打電話跟瀏覽網頁的話，可以用兩天不需要充電。
Adam	It sounds awesome. What else is worthy of emphasizing about this battery?	聽起來真的很棒。這顆電池還有其他值得一題之處嗎？

| Wendy | This battery is quiet **durable**. According to the data from the testing lab, it can recharge for more than 3000 times. | 這顆電池超耐用，根據測試室的數據，它可以充電超過3000次。 |
| Adam | After your brief introductions of this battery, I am so excited to see the finished product soon. | 聽完妳們簡單對手機電池的介紹後，我很期待趕快看到成品。 |

C 對話單字、片語說分明

① **development** *n.* 發展

例 The development of this software faced has almost no bottleneck.

這套軟體在開發過程中幾乎沒碰到任何瓶頸。

② **achievement** *n.* 成就

例 Looking back to the achievement I have made in the one month, getting the order from ABV Company is the greatest one.

回顧過去一個月所達到的成就，獲得ABV公司的訂單是最棒的那個。

③ **simplified** *v.* 簡化

例 This application procedure is too complicated, so I have asked Mary to simplify it within three working days.

此申請程序太過複雜，所以我已要求瑪莉於三個工作天將其簡化。

④ **instruction** *n.* 指令

例 The bugs result from the wrong instruction, so now our engineers are modifying it.

有漏洞是因為指令出錯，所以目前我們的工程師正在修正指令中。

⑤ **necessity** *n.* 必需品

例 Internet has become one of the necessities in our life.

網路已成為我們的生活必需品之一。

⑥ **inevitably** *adv.* 無可避免地

例 Since this machine has many customized parts, so the price is inevitably higher than that of the mass production one.

由於此機器包含許多客製設計，價格就無可避免地會比大量生產的款式貴。

⑦ **durable** *adj.* 耐用的

例 The greatest strength of our product is durable.

我們產品最大的優點就是耐用。

D 換句話說補一補

I have broken the back of the automatic bug detecting
我已經克服自動偵錯的難關了。

★ I **have overcome the most difficult part about** the automatic bug detecting.

★ I have **found the know-how of** the automatic bug detecting.

 解析時間

① **have overcome the most difficult part about**

 have overcome the most difficult part about意思是「已經克服最……困難的部分」。當某項工作的困難已經找到解決之道，其他的部分處理起來就相對輕鬆。因此，當未來我們成功地解決某項工作中最艱難之處時，就可以用We have overcome the most difficult part of/about...來振奮士氣。

② **found the know-how of**

解析 found the know-how of...意思是「找到……的箇中巧妙」。Know-how指的就是各種領域的關鍵技術，若掌握此技術，方可獲得領先地位。根據此邏輯，未來如果我們在工作過程中發現某種方法可以每次幾乎都事半功倍，就可以借用know-how一詞，以We have found the know-how of ...來自我激勵。

Living in an Information Age, most consumers **can't bear waiting too long for** the answer or outcome they need.

生在資訊世代，多數的消費者沒有耐心花太多時間等他們需要的答案或結果。

★ Living in an Information Age, most consumers **don't have much patience to wait for** the answer or outcome they need.

★ Living in an Information Age, most consumers **want to know** the answer or outcome they need **as soon as possible**.

 解析時間

① **don't have much patience to wait for**

解析 don't have much patience to wait for 意思是「不太有耐心等…」。換句話說，久等無疑是在挑戰他或她的極限。因此，當我們要提醒同事某個客戶性子很急時，就可以用Sb. don't have much patience to wait for...來表示。

② **want to know ... as soon as possible**

解析 want to know... as soon as possible意思是「想要盡快知道……」。當某人凡事都想趕快知道結果，代表此人也是急性子。因此，不管此人是你主管還是客戶，都可以用since sb. wants to know... as soon as possible, I...來提醒自己處理事情的速度記得要快。

Traditionally, the volume **is directly proportional to thickness.** 電池容量與厚度成正比。

★ Traditionally, **the higher the volume is, the thicker the thickness is.**

★ Traditionally, **the volume decides the thickness of the battery.**

 解析時間

① **The 比較級 the N is, the 比較級 the N is.**

解析 The 比較級 the N is, the 比較級 the N is意思是「N 越……，N就越……」，可用於說明兩件事物的關聯性。如果是正相關，比較級往正面意涵走，如果是負相關，就往負面意涵走。舉例來說，當你發現價錢越低，銷售情況越好，就可以這麼說：the cheaper the price is, the better the sales figure is。

② **The N1 decides the N2 of the...**

解析 The N1 decides the N2 of the...意思是「N1決定了N2 的……」，在概念上強調N1的重要性。因此當我們在開會中要把表達某一要素的重要性時，例如知名度影響購買慾就可以 用The brand awareness decides the desire of the purchase來表示。

E 非學不可的職場小貼示

對話中所出現的R&D一字是research & development的縮寫，意思是研發，是科技業很常見的一個單字。但很多人在念這個字的時候，會把中間的&（讀做and）拿掉，變成RD。這樣的省略看似差異不大，但事實上會讓外國人一頭霧水。

會產生誤會的原因在有人會把自己的姓與名的首字母縮寫作為簡稱。舉知名的籃球員Michael Jordan可自稱MJ。因此若R&D變成RD，會讓人誤會以為在叫某人，而不是稱呼整個團隊。

理解這層差異後，往後稱呼研發團隊時，可千萬別再偷懶了，不然大家溝通了半天，對方還是沒弄懂你想表達的意思。

Part 2 〔內勤〕辦公室會議篇

Unit 12 Shoot from the hip
不經考慮就說與做

 A 辭彙文化背景介紹

如果單看字面，shoot from the hip 意思是「從臀部開槍」。乍聽之下，我們可能還找不出臀部跟開槍的關聯性，但如果把時間回推到美國的西部拓荒時期，這一切就會非常合理。

一講到拓荒時期，大家首先想到的就是牛仔。由於可能碰到猛獸襲擊，或是必須與人決鬥，牛仔都會隨身帶槍自保。那牛仔的槍都放在哪邊呢？為求能夠快速拔槍，牛仔的槍套大多放在臀部附近，但如果拔槍後沒有瞄準隨意開槍，雖然搶得先機但卻不見得可以克敵制勝，因此 shoot from the hip 後來就引申為「不經思考就⋯⋯」。

雖然不經思考就做事聽起來很負面，但反應相對直接，且回應迅速，故仍有可取之處。因此，未來在工作上如果發現自己的同事做事反應很快，但常常思考欠周延時，就可以用 don't shoot from the hip 來提醒他／她。

看看辭彙怎麼用

【同事間】Between colleagues

Patty 珮緹	About the market **segmentation** of our new product, I have had a meeting with Lucy and all the other colleagues of the International Sales Department this morning, and I felt she tended to **give me a tit for tart** during the meeting.	關於新產品的市場區隔，我早上與露西跟其他國貿部同事開過會，會間我覺得露西刻意與我針鋒相對。
Daisy 黛西	Lucy is a straightforward person, so I believe she doesn't mean to **embarrass** you. Could you briefly re-illustrate what you two just went over?	露西個性直接，所以我覺得她應該不是刻意要讓你難堪。你可以簡單重述剛剛的討論內容嗎？
Patty	Sure. Since our new product is fashionable and **delicate**, I assume that the consumer around 30 to 40 is the group that has the highest purchase power. However, Lucy just criticizes me that I have a wrong judgment.	當然可以。因為我們的新產品新潮且精緻，我認為30到40歲的消費者最具有購買力，但露西批評說我判斷錯誤。

Daisy　In my opinion, <u>Lucy shoots from the hip about this</u>. Lucy is young, so she thinks only the youth has great interest in modern stuff. What's more, Her negligence of the price is another deciding factor. The consumers under 30 may have the intent to buy our product, but later they will find the price is somehow not affordable.

就我看來，露西沒想清楚就批評你。露西她還很年輕，所以她想說只有年輕人對新潮的東西有興趣。此外，她也忽略掉價格的因素。30歲以下的消費者可能會有購買的欲望，但往往會覺得這樣的價格有點太高。

Patty　After your explanation, I feel much relieved now. I will find some time to talk to Lucy about this privately.

經過你的一番解釋後，我覺得舒坦許多了。我會再找時間私下跟露西重述剛剛的內容。

【主管與屬下間】
Between the supervisor and the employee

Patrick
派翠克　The topic we have to go over today is the deal with KIH Company. I have heard that we haven't received the down payment. Can anyone give me a brief explanation and the **feasible** follow-ups?

我們今天開會的主題是關於KIH公司。我聽說現在還沒收到尾款。有人可以簡單說明一下原因以及可行的後續處理嗎？

Randy
蘭迪

As I know, KIH faces an unexpected funding gap now. However, I think all companies know that all investments have certain risks. We shall send KIH the first **collection** letter now.

就我所知，KIH目前出現意外的資金缺口。但我認為所有公司都了解投資必有風險。現在我們應該第一次向KIH催款。

Wallace
華勒斯

You are 100 percent right from the legal perspective, but you somehow shoot from the hip in this case. We have been cooperated with KIH for years, so we could give them some flexibility. I suggest that the deadline can be set on this Friday. If KIH still fail to pay, we have no choice but to ask for compensation.

從法律面來看，你的做法完全沒錯。但這個做法的思考有欠周延。我們已經跟KIH合作多年，所以我建議給他們一點彈性。付款的最後期限可以設在這星期五。如果KIH到時後還時沒付款，在要求賠償。

Patrick

I totally agree. Being a partner with KIH, we can empathize they are facing some difficulties. Meanwhile, being a member of ABC Company, we can't **stand aside** when our company has the chance to lose money.

我完全同意。做為KIH的商業夥伴，我們可以體會他們正遭逢困難。但做為ABC公司的一份子，同樣不能坐看公司可能虧損，但卻袖手旁觀。

| Randy | I am convinced. I should think more thoroughly next time. | 我也被說服了。下次我會思考的更周延些。 |
| Patrick | It seems we have reached a consensus in what to do next. Let's warp it up here. | 看來大家都已經知道接下來該怎麼做,散會。 |

對話單字、片語說分明

① **segmentation** *ph.* 區隔

例 The success of this crossover product comes from its clear market segmentation.

此聯名商品的成功來自於清楚的市場區隔。

② **give me a tit for tart** *ph.* 與……針鋒相對

例 I feel Jane gives me a tit for tart in the direction of our marketing strategy.

我覺得珍在行銷策略這件事上與我針鋒相對。

③ **embarrass** *v.* 使……難堪

例 I don't mean to embarrass you. What I just said is the conclusion of my observation from your performance in the past few months.

我沒有刻意要讓你難堪，剛才所說的都是根據我對你過去數個月的表現的觀察所總結而來。

④ **delicate** *adj.* 精緻的

（例） The delicate appearance is the greatest strength of this smartphone.

這款智慧型手機的最大賣點就是外型精緻。

⑤ **feasible** *adj.* 可行的

（例） Pay more freight is one of the feasible solutions in this case.

在本次情況下，多付運費是可行的方法之一。

⑥ **collection** *n.* 催款

（例） Since the buyer delayed the payment, I have sent the collection letter.

由於買方欠款，我已寄出催款信。

⑦ **stand aside** *ph.* 袖手旁觀

（例） We shouldn't stand aside when our company faces fierce challenge.

公司有難時我們不該袖手旁觀。

D 換句話說補一補

Lucy is a **straightforward** person, so I believe she doesn't mean to embarrass you.

露西個性直接，所以我覺得她應該不是刻意要讓你難堪。

★ Lucy **doesn't beat around the bush**, so I believe she doesn't...

★ Lucy **doesn't play tricks**, so I believe she doesn't...

 解析時間

① **doesn't beat around the bush**

解析 doesn't beat around the bush意思是「不拐彎抹角」。這個慣用語源於獵人靠拍打樹叢使驚嚇獵物，以方便狩獵。後來衍生出不直接做某事的意涵。在職場上，若有人想刻意閃躲某個議題，會故意言之無物，這時你就可以用Please don't beat around the bush 提醒對方趕快切入正題。

② **doesn't play tricks**

解析 doesn't play tricsk意思是「不耍手段」。個性直接或正直的人通常有話就直說，不會工於心計去耍手段。因此，當我們在職場上要稱讚他人為人直接了當時，就可以用sb. don't play tricks來表示。

Since our new product is fashionable and delicate, I **assume** that the consumer around 30 to 40 is the group that has the highest purchase power.

因為我們的新產品新潮且精緻，我認為30到40歲的消費者最具有購買力。

★ Since our new product...,the consumer around 30 to 40 **would be** the group that has the highest purchase power **from my point of view**.

★ Since our new product..., I **wildly guess** that the consumer around 30 to 40 is the group that has the highest purchase power.

 解析時間

① **N would be ...from my point of view**

解析 N would be ...from my point of view意思是「從我的觀點看，N會是……」。不論是支持或是反對，皆可以此句型可用於表述自身觀點，因此，如果在會議過程你想針對某個議題或是論點表示意見時，就可以N would be ...from my point of view來表示。

② **wildly guess**

解析 wildly guess意思是「大膽猜測」。雖說是猜測，但其實也有所本，故本用法也可與「認為」互做替換。因此，未來當你在開會中，若想延伸論點，就可以用I wildly guess that...來表示。

Meanwhile, being a member of ABC Company, we can't **stand aside** when our company has the chance to lose money. 做為ABC公司的一份子，同樣不能坐看公司可能虧損，但卻袖手旁觀。

★ Meanwhile, being a member of ABC Company, we can't **do nothing but witness that** our company has the chance to lose money.

★ Meanwhile, being a member of ABC Company, we **should stand out when** our company has the chance to lose money.

 解析時間

① **do nothing but witness...**

解析 do nothing but witness... 意思是「眼睜睜看著……」，表示某人明明知道某事（通常是壞事）將發生，卻毫無作為。因此，當我們要呼籲同事間一起努力度過難關時，就可以用負負得正的方式，以we can't do nothing but witness... 來表達。

② **Sb. should stand out when...**

解析 should stand out when... 意思是「當……時某人應當挺身而出」。此用法的呼籲性最強，因此不論你是做為主管還是員工，當要在會議中激勵士氣，讓所有人目標一致時，就可以用We should stand out when... 來表示。

E 非學不可的職場小貼示

　　看到collection這個單字，相信大家都先想到它有「蒐集」的意思。那如果是在商業領域中，collection還是相同意思嗎？從本單元的對話，答案是否。collection在貿易領域中指的是催款。但這個陌生的意涵，只不過是在想法上多轉了個彎，現在就來跟大家說明整個衍生過程。在買賣過程中，對賣方而言最重要的是收到錢，所以當收不到錢時，就會跟買方討，而討錢的過程就跟我們蒐集某種事物一樣，需要花點功夫與時間。透過這樣的邏輯推演，相信你也記住為何collection也可以叫催款了吧！

Unit 13 | Corner the market
壟斷市場

 A 辭彙文化背景介紹

　　即使懂得英文單字不多，不少人仍然知道 corner 如果當名詞使用，意思是「角落」。但如果把 corner 當成動詞，可能大家就非常陌生了，但事實上，只要想像自己正身處角落，就很容易理解為何可以有此解釋。

　　現在就請大家想像自己是位拳擊手，你正與對手公平較量。當你把對手逼到角落，由於不能超出比賽場地範圍，在此情況下你掌握了大部分的優勢，此時只要抓住機會給予重擊，就有機會贏得比賽。相反地，如果是你被逼到角落，就要想辦法脫身，否則只有挨打的份。

　　若把商場上的競爭視作一種拚搏，當我們把競爭對手逼到角落，就代表對於整個市場的控制度獲得提升。而在經過幾番交手後，若將對手成功撂倒，也就代表我們完全掌控市場，因此 corner the market 的意思就是「壟斷市場」。

B 看看辭彙怎麼用

【同事間】Between colleagues

Alex
艾力克斯

Hey, Johnson, next Tuesday is the seasonal meeting, how's your market observation?

嘿,強森,下星期二就要開季會了,你的市場觀察狀況如何?

Johnson
強森

After a six-month **investigation**, I find one thing worthy of discussing in the meeting. That is, we have a **tough** challenger, NBP in the market. Though it is a new brand in sport apparel and shoes, its growth astonishes me. The sales double within six months.

經過六個月的調查,我發現一件很值得在會議中提出的事。就是市場上出現一個強悍的挑戰者NBP了。雖然他是在運動鞋與服飾市場中的後起之秀,但它的成長速度令我驚訝。才六個月就以業績翻倍。

Alex

I think you overestimate its impact to us. <u>Upon viewing the market share, we still corner the market.</u> Maybe you should **shift** the focus of the observation to our main competitor PLF from next quarter because PLF's new running shoes just won many positive feedbacks from the users not long ago.

我覺得你高估了NBP的影響力。單看市佔率,我們仍舊獨占鰲頭。或許下一季你該把觀察的重點轉移到我們最主要的競爭對手PLF身上,因為不久前他們所推出的新跑鞋,獲得許多跑者的正面評價。

Johnson	It could be right, but knowing who is challenging our **dominating** position does no harm. I still find it necessary to report this change in the market to our boss.	也許你說的是對的，但多了解有誰正在挑戰我們的領導地位有益而無害。我覺得還是應該向老闆報告市場上所出現的這個變化。
Alex	In such sense, I agree. As the marketing specialist, keeping an eye on all the challengers in the market is our duties.	如果從這個角度看的話，我同意。做為行銷專員，留意市場上所有的挑戰者是我們的職責所在。

【主管與屬下間】

Between the supervisor and the employee

Ben 班	Next year we are scheduled to enter Canada market, what do you find in the market survey, Peterson?	我們預計明年進軍加拿大市場，請問彼得森你從市場研究中有發現什麼嗎？
Peterson 彼得森	<u>OLK is the leading brand of casual apparel in this market because its 55 percent market shares have cornered the market.</u>	由於市佔率高達百分之五十五，OLK是這個市場休閒服飾的領導品牌。

	Besides, OLK targets the middle class, so finding another war field seems necessary if we want to stand firmly in the market soon.	此外，該品牌主打中產階級，如果我們想要趕快站穩腳步，可能得另闢戰場。
Ben	Have you come up with some ideas about the product positioning?	你有想到該怎樣定位我們的產品了嗎？
Peterson	Since OLK has reached the economies of scale, we have no competitiveness in cost alone. However, there is a great demand in the customization from consumers in the top of the **pyramid**. The need of this group could be a **promising** market for us. Because this group is more willing to pay more to become unique, the **revenue** we could generate from them is great. What's more, the design is different from time to time and quantity is relatively small per patch, so the inventory won't bother us.	因為OLK已達規模經濟，單就成本而言，我們毫無競爭力。但在消費金字塔頂端有相當大的客製需求。此族群的需求會是個有前景的市場。由於此族群願意多付點錢來使自己看起來獨特，我們能從他們身上賺到不少錢。此外，因為每批的設計都不同，且生產數量相對少，所以不會有存貨過多的困擾。

Ben	Your suggestion looks workable. Each product has its niche market, finding where it is at the very beginning matters.	你的建議似乎可行。每個產品都有其利基市場，有沒有在一開始就找出事關重大。
Peterson	Right. Later I will integrate all the information I have gathered and give you a more specific presentation tomorrow.	沒錯。等下我會整合我收集到的資料，明天跟你做更詳細的報告。

 對話單字、片語說分明

① **investigation** *n.* 調查

例 To find out the reason of the drop in sales, we conduct a two-month investigation.

為找出銷售衰退的原因，我們進行為期兩個月的調查。

② **tough** *adj.* 強悍的

例 Now we are ready to face the tough challenge in the smartphone market.

我們已經準備好面對在智慧型手機市場的強力挑戰。

③ **shift** *v.* 改變

例 The marketing strategy shall be shifted according to the market trend.
行銷策略應當依照市場趨勢做改變。

④ **dominating** *adj.* 主宰的

例 Since ABC Company gains the most market share, it is hard to challenge its dominating position in the market.
由於ABC公司擁有最高市佔率，要撼動其主宰地位難上加難。

⑤ **pyramid** *n.* 金字塔

例 Though the population of consumers from the top of the pyramid is small, its purchase power is great.
雖然金字塔頂端消費者的人口數少，但其消費力高。

⑥ **promising** *adj.* 有前景的

例 Producing solar cells could be a promising industry in the coming fifty years.
太陽能電池在接下來的50年會是一個大有前途的產業。

⑦ **revenue** *n.* 收入

例 To generate more revenue, we should develop some fashion items.
為了要有更多收入，我們應該開發潮流商品。

D 換句話說補一補

Upon viewing the market share, we still **corner the market**.
單看市佔率，我們仍舊獨占鰲頭。

★ Upon viewing the market share, we still **gain the most market shares**.

★ Upon viewing the market share, we **are still the most beloved brand**.

★ Upon viewing the market share, we still **take the lead in** the market.

 解析時間

① **gain the most market shares**

　解析　gain the most market shares意思是「市佔率最高」。產品的市佔率越高，其市場領先地位越明顯。

② **are still the most beloved brand**

　解析　are still the most beloved brand意思是「仍為最受喜愛品牌」。此一用法表現出雖然我們現在仍榮膺第一，但後方已有追兵正在趕上。因此在會議中，如果覺得自家公司表現良好，但市場中已有新秀崛起時，就可以用we are still the most beloved brand, but...來表示。

③ **take the lead in...**

　解析　take the lead in...意思是「在……中居於領先」，如果在商

138

業競爭上居於領先，其產品市佔率肯定也高。因此，當我們在會議要表達公司某項產品表現居於同業之冠時，就可以用…take the lead in... 來表示。

As the marketing specialist, **keeping an eye on** all the challengers in the market is our duties.
做為行銷專員，留意市場上所有的挑戰者是我們的職責所在。

★ As the marketing specialist, **knowing the current status of** all the challenger in the market is our duties.

★ As the marketing specialist, **being aware of the situation of** all the challengers in the market is our duties.

★ As the marketing specialist, **updating the information about** all the challenger in the market is our duties.

 解析時間

① **know the current status of**

解析 know the current status of... 意思是「了解……的近況」。在商場上若能得知對手的近況，要做出對應的處置也較容易。

② **be aware of the situation of**

解析 be aware of the situation of 意思是「留意……的情況」。在商場上若有注意對方的變化，知己知彼百戰不殆。因此，當在會議中要表達調查對手的重要性，就可以用if we are aware of situation of ...., then we... 這類的句型表示。

③ update the information about

解析 update the information about... 意思是「更新關於…的資訊」。在商場上，若能隨時留意市場最新資訊，就能比對手更快嗅到商機。因此若要在開會中表達更新訊息的重要性，就可以用 we should update the information about... 來表示。

The need of this group could be **a promising market** for us.
此族群的需求會是個有前景的市場。

★ The need of this group could be **a market with great potential** for us.

★ The need of this group could be a **booming** market for us.

★ The need of this group could **generate many business opportunities** for us.

 解析時間

① a market with great potential

解析 a market with great potential 意思是「是個有潛力的市場」。此用法在語氣上稍微含蓄，但目的還是要凸顯產品有前景。因此，當在會議中要表述此類情況時，就可以用 The...of...could be a market with potential to us 來表示。

② booming

解析 booming 意思是「蓬勃發展的」。一個發展快速的市場，前景

相對看好，因此booming與promising在語意上其實可以互作替換。如在開會過程中，想表達產品銷售狀況走高，且有望繼續保持，就可以用The product has a booming market來表示。

③ **generate many business opportunities**

解析 generate many business opportunities意思是「創造許多商機」。當市場有前景時，商機自然不會少，因此，在會議中若要表達某項產品很有發展性時，就可以用...can generate many business opportunities來表示。

E 非學不可的職場小貼示

　　本單元的兩篇對話都與市佔率(market share)有關，因此這邊簡單說明市佔率所代表的意涵，以及該如何於商用對話中使用此單字。Market share中的share一字指的就是「一小份」。若把整個市場當成一大塊派，每家公司的產品就像是當中的一部分。如果份數越多，被消費者選到的機會就越高。

Part 2 【內勤】辦公室會議篇

Unit 14 Thorny issue 棘手問題

A 辭彙文化背景介紹

在解釋thorny issue的意思之前，要先理解thorn這個單字。Thorn指的是「刺」或「荊棘」，所以thorny就是「有刺的」。依照這樣邏輯，我們就會把thorny issue翻成「有刺的議題」。

但有刺的議題指的何種議題，還是讓人有點一頭霧水。所以這邊用一個小小比喻來跟大家說明。假設今天我們的手指被植物的刺刺到，如果刺得很深，就會產生兩種問題，一是處理起來有難度，二是不處理會產生後續問題。根據相同的邏輯思維，如果有件事不容易處理，但卻不能丟著不管，這種事就叫做thorny issue。

在職場上，除了例行會議外，很多會議都是針對有緊急性的議題而召開，這樣的會議主題就可以被稱作thorny issue。所以下次有機會參與此類會議時，就可以於會議一開始時說we will discuss a thorny issue today。

看看辭彙怎麼用

【同事間】Between colleagues

Vivian 薇薇安	Hi, Shelly, can you give me a hand now?	嗨,雪莉。可以幫我一個忙嗎?
Shelly 雪莉	Sure, how can I help you?	當然可以,要怎麼幫你呢?
Vivian	Checking the inventory **in hand**, and print it out.	查詢目前的存貨數量,然後把報表印出來。
Shelly	What's going on? Those figures are usually reviewed once at the end of every single month, but you want them now.	發生什麼事了?這些數據通常每個月底才會檢核一次,但現在你就跟我要這些資訊了。

Vivian	Tell you a **breaking** news. The freighter that carries our machines sank yesterday due to its mechanical **malfunction**, making us have no choice but to find a supplement of this patch. Now, I think you already have the idea why I ask you to check the spare items. <u>The whole international sales team will have a meeting concerning this thorny issue one hour later.</u>	跟你說個震撼的消息。載有本公司機器的貨輪昨天因為自身機械故障而沉沒，所以我們只能尋找別的機器來代替這批貨。一小時後，國貿團隊邀針對這個棘手情況開會。
	(Vivian checks the system and gets the figure of each warehouse worldwide.)	（薇薇安查詢系統後獲得全球各地倉庫的數據。）
Vivian	Considering the transportation time and the quantity, dispatching the inventory in Germany or Holland is a good option. Though we have paid extra freight, but the insurance will cover these **expenses**.	考量到交通時間跟數量充足與否，調度在荷蘭或是德國的存貨是優先選擇。雖然需要多付運費，但保險金就能抵銷這些支出。
Shelly	Good job Vivian. Just repeat what you just told me in the meeting later.	做得好，薇薇安。等等開會就重複一遍你剛說的內容吧！

【主管與屬下間】

Between the supervisor and the employee

Bruno
布魯諾

Jack, please make sure the main conference room is **available** or not this morning because President Jason and CLO Carl will arrive one hour later.

傑克，請確認大會議室今天早上是沒人使用的，因為一小時後傑森董事長跟法務長卡爾會來。

Jack
傑克

They rarely comes to this office unless there's a thorny issue, so could I ask what happened?

除非有棘手事件發生，否則他們很少過來。所以可以請問到底發生什麼事了？

Bruno

We both know who Vincent is, right! He is the senior sales representative in our team, and his performance has been good for long. However, he is suspected of revealing our **confidential** information to our competitors and got commissions last week after the investigation made by our legal department. We have to take actions before he notices, and that's why our boss comes here without informing.

我們都知道文生是誰，他是本團隊資深業務，一直以來表現都很優良。但經過本公司法務部門調查後，發現他上週涉嫌洩漏公司機密給競爭對手，並從中取得佣金。公司必須在其查覺前，搶先採取行動，而這也是老闆不通知就過來的原因。

Jack	I see. Since I have the authorization to review the internal data accessing, I can get his record as proof of his **theft**.	我了解了。因為我有權限檢視內部系統存取狀況，我可以調出紀錄證明他有竊取資料之實。
Bruno	Good job. I will transfer this message to the President Special Secretary. If our boss needs this document, just print it out.	做得好。我會把此訊息轉達給總裁特助。如果老闆需要這份文件，就印出來。

C 對話單字、片語說分明

① **in hand** *ph.* 在手邊的

例 What's the total of the spare goods we have in hand now?
我們目前手邊的備品總數有多少呢？

② **breaking** *adj.* 突發的

例 The bankruptcy of ANM Company is a breaking news.
ANM 公司的破產對我來說一大震撼消息。

③ **malfunction** *n.* 故障

例 Due to malfunction in production line this morning, we are behind the schedule now.

因為早上生產線出現故障，我們現在進度落後了。

④ **expenses** *n.* 花費

例 All the expenses of this marketing campaign shall be controlled in 10,000 USD.

本次行銷活動的所有花費應控制在1萬美金。

⑤ **available** *adj.* 有空的

例 When will you be available to have a meeting with me this afternoon?

今天下午你何時有空跟我開會呢？

⑥ **confidential** *adj.* 機密的

例 Unless you get the authorization, or you can't review the confidential information.

除非獲得授權，否則你無法檢視機密資料。

⑦ **theft** *n.* 偷竊

例 He is accused of theft of confidential documents.

他被以竊取機密資料的罪名起訴。

D 換句話說補一補

Hi, Shelly, can you **give me a hand now**?
嗨，雪莉。可以幫我一個忙嗎？
★ Hi, Shelly, can you **do me a favor**now?
★ Hi, Shelly, **would you mind helping me** now?
★ Hi, Shelly, **are you free to help me** now?

 解析時間

① **Do me a favor**

解析 do me a favor意思是「幫我個忙」，在語意上與give me a hand 相近。若真的細分兩者的差異，favor的帶有較多懇求語氣。因此，未來在工作上，如果需要別人給予協助時，就可以選擇上述兩種用法。

② **Would you mind helping me**

解析 Would you mind helping me意思「是介不介意幫我個忙」，在語氣上又更加客氣。一般來說，當對方如此有禮貌地詢問，被請求的一方通常都肯伸出援手。

③ **Are you free to help me**

解析 Are you free to help me意思是「你有空幫我嗎」。此用法隱含如果對方沒空，不幫忙也沒關係的意思，在語氣上也十分客氣。因此，下次如果發現同事手邊也有工作，但自己確實需要他／她的協助時，就可以are you free to help me來加以詢問。

However, he is suspected of revealing our **confidential information** to our competitors and got commissions last week after the investigation made by our legal department.

★ However, he is suspected of revealing our **confidentiality** to our competitors and got commissions last week...

★ However, he is suspected of revealing our **business secrets** to our competitors and got commissions last week...

 解析時間

① **confidentiality**

解析 confidentiality 意思是「機密」。機密指的就是不能隨意公開的資訊，因此在職場上若沒有獲得權限，切記不要隨意存取或是散布機密，以免惹禍上身。當要表達自己無權得知某項機密文件內容時就可以用 I am not authorized to access this confidentiality 來表示。

② **business secret**

解析 business secret 意思是「商業機密」。公司的商業機密一旦外流，將可能面臨鉅額損失。因此，在職場上如果有人試圖從你身上得知公司的機密，就可以用 this is business secret, so no commend.（這是商業機密，所以無可奉告）來加以回絕。

Since I have the authorization to review the internal data accessing, I can get his record as proof of his **theft**.

因為我有權限檢視內部系統存取狀況，我可以調出紀錄證明他有竊取資料之實。

★ Since I have..., I can get his record to prove he **has the intent to steal and he really does it**.

★ Since I have..., I can get his record as the proof of his **illegal information acquiring**.

 解析時間

① **has the intent to steal and sbreally does it**

解析 has the intent to steal and sb.really does it意思是「有偷竊意圖且真的下手了」。此用法著重意圖的表述，因此相當適合作為陳述某一行為的發生，而本單元舉負面行為作範例。但此句型也可用於描述職場上的正面行為，例如當你想分析資料且真的行動了，就可以用 I have the intent to analyze and I really do it來表示。

② **illegal information acquiring**

解析 illegal information acquiring 意思是「非法資訊獲取」，換言之就是偷取資訊。由於這樣的用法特別強調該行為的不合法性，因此上司要提醒下屬遵守資安規定時，就可用 Please don't have any illegal information acquiring來表示。

E 非學不可的職場小貼示

　　在本單元對話中，有出現一個大家可能不是這樣熟悉的職位名稱，就是CLO，CLO是Chief Legal Officer的縮寫，意思就是法務長，而法務長的最重要職掌就是公司的法律事務。

　　此類型的職務，其實在組成邏輯上概念都相同，皆採「位階＋職掌＋官銜」的組合，以法務長為例，chief就代表處為最高位階，legal代表要處理法律問題，而officer就是其官銜。因此若要解是什麼叫法務長，就是處理公司法律問題的最高層人員。

　　經過上面的簡單解釋，相信大家就可以類推CIO、CKO、COO等「長」字輩的業務範圍到底在哪了。

Unit 15 Play cards right 處理得當

A 辭彙文化背景介紹

　　如果直譯play cards right，意思就是「出正確的牌」。講到這邊，大家覺得這個慣用法應該十之八九與撲克牌有關。沒錯，這個用法真的源於打牌時的一個基本邏輯。

　　只要玩過撲克牌的人都知道，不小心打錯一張牌，可能接下來的牌局都不順。相反地，如果打出對的牌，一手好牌的人可以乘勝追擊，一手爛牌的人可以反敗為勝。若把商業競爭是做一場牌局，打對牌就代表「處置得當」，而這也是play cards right的真正意涵。

　　由於本用法的card意思接近手邊的資源。所以一定有good card跟bad card。但不論手牌好壞，善用其特性才是重點。因此，當我們要在會議中強調某個環節務必要處理好，以避免衍生事端時，就可以用Make sure you play cards right, or... 來表示。

看看辭彙怎麼用

【同事間】**Between colleagues**

Andrew 安卓	Since we have too many consumer complaints this month, our manager, Mr. Lin decides to have a meeting this afternoon. What kind of circumstances have you encountered so far?	這個月我們被客訴太多次了，所以林經理下午要開會檢討，你目前有處理過那些狀況了？
Hank 漢克	I have received countless e-mails about the problem of **coupon**. The contents all indicate that the link in our official website doesn't work, so they can't download the file to their phone or **pad**. Another thing is wrong pricing of hair drier. The discounted price shall be 25 USD but we make it 2.5 USD by mistake. Many consumers placed the order and received the failure message sent by the system later.	我收到很多關於優惠券的客訴。那些信件內容都是在講官網上的連結是無效的，所以她們不能把優惠券下載到手機或是平板。另外一個是吹風機標錯價。本來的優惠價是25美金，但卻誤植為2.5美金。許多消費者下單後沒多久就收到系統發出的交易失敗訊息。

Part 2

【內勤】辦公室會議篇

Andrew	Both cases sound serious. What is your reply?	兩個問題聽起來都很嚴重。你是怎麼回覆消費者的呢？
Hank	Firstly, I showed the most sincere **apology** for our mistake. Secondly, I explained the reason of the malfunction of the link. And lastly, I pointed out that ABC Company will send a special coupon to those who have placed an order as the compensation. Besides, to show our appreciation to all consumers, I also released the news of an extra special sale on our website.	首先，我先對錯誤表達誠摯歉意。接下來我針對連結無效的原因做解釋。最後，我告知來信者ABC公司會對已經下單的消費者給予特別優惠券做為補償。此外，為表達對消費者的感謝，我也在官網上釋出將有額外特賣的訊息。
Andrew	You do play cards right. If I were the consumer, I will be **satisfied** with your answer.	你的處置很到位。如果是消費者，這樣的回覆我可以接受。

【主管與屬下間】

Between the supervisor and the employee

Nick 尼克	Why we have the meeting today is that BAF tends to cancel the order this time.	今天要開會是因為這次 BAF 想要取消下單。
Franklin 富蘭克林	I just received the confirmation of types and quantity yesterday, so how come the situation **reversed**?	我昨天才剛他們確認型號與數量，為何情況整個翻轉了？
Nick	As I know, such change results from the budget control of **logistics**. The cutting in storage fees makes them stop the renting of one warehouse, so they tend to postpone order in case they find no room to store the goods.	就我所知，會有這樣的變化是因為物流的預算改變。倉儲費刪減迫使得少租一個倉庫，所以 BAF 想要延後下單以避免出現貨物沒地方放的情況產生。
Franklin	If that were the reason, I have a good idea. Can the shipping of an order be divided into several patches according to our company policy?	如果這就是真正原因的話，我這邊有個解決方法。根據公司政策，一張訂單可以分批出貨嗎？

Nick	As long as an extra provision is written in the order, the answer is yes.	只要訂單中有載明就可以。
Franklin	I got it. Since shipping by patch works, informing BAF this option could be a good way to finalize this deal. If you agree, then I can **initiate** the follow-ups after the meeting.	我了解了。因為分批出貨可行,將此訊息告知BAF似乎是加速成交的好方法。如果你同意,會後我就開始執行後續。
Nick	<u>I think you can play cards rightin this case, so just do it.</u>	我相信你可以把這件事處理得很好,就放手去做吧!

C 對話單字、片語說分明

① **coupon** *ph.* 優惠券

例 With this coupon, you can save up to 25percent.
如使用此優惠券,最多讓你打七五折。

② **pad** *n.* 平板

例 For many sales, pads have replaced notebooks as the handy equipment to have presentations to the clients.

對許多業務來說，平板已經取代筆電成為他們向客戶簡報時的最便利設備。

③ **apology** *n.* 道歉

例 Please acceptmy apology for my carelessness in time arrangement.

對於時間安排上的疏忽我深表歉意。

④ **satisfied** *adj.* 滿意的

例 Since you notice the details, I feel satisfied with your service.

由於你有注意到細節，我對你的服務感到滿意。

⑤ **reverse** *v.* 翻轉

例 The inflation reverses the economy in this region.

通貨膨脹使此區域的經濟情況急轉直下。

⑥ **logistics** *n.* 物流

例 To save the logistics fee, we ship two patches of product at a time.

為節省物流費，我們兩批貨一起出貨。

⑦ **initiate** *v.* 開始

例 When receiving the permission from my boss, I can initiate this project.

一旦我獲得老闆的許可，我就可以開始執行此專案。

D 換句話說補一補

Besides, to **show our appreciation to** all consumers, I also release the news of an extra special sale on our website.
此外，為表達對消費者的感謝，我也在官網上釋出將有額外特賣的訊息。

★ Besides, to **give** all consumers **the most direct feedback**, I also release the news of an extra special sale on our website.

★ Besides, to show our **thankfulness** to all consumers, I also release the news of an extra special sale on our website.

★ Besides, **to give** all consumers **more favors**, I also release the news of an extra special sale on our website.

 解析時間

① **give sb. the most direct feedback**

解析 give sb. the most direct feedback 意思是「給予……最直接的回饋」。若從賣方的立場看，給予客戶最直接的回饋就是打折，因此當在會議中討論到要如何感謝消費者時，就可以用 To give our client the most direct feedback,... 來表示。

② **thankfulness**

解析 thankfulness 意思是「感激」，在語意上與 appreciation 相近。在商場上，感激客戶的方式有很多，例如免運費、打折、

滿額贈等等，因此若要會議中表達希望透過某種方式回饋客戶時，就可以用To show our thankfulness, we... 來表示。

③ **to give sb. more favors**

解析 to give sb. more favors意思是「給予……更多優惠」。就回饋客戶的角度看，打折最實際，但也有人喜歡拿贈品。因此當你在會議中想要強調此論點時，就可以用To give our customer more favor is an good option來表示。

You do play cards right. If I were the consumer, I will be satisfied with your answer.

如果是消費者，這樣的回覆我可以接受。

★ You do **make things come to a good end**. If I were the consumer, I...

★ You **truly know what we consumers want**. If I were the consumer, I...

★ You do **get consumers' point**. If I were the consumer, I...

 解析時間

① **make ... come to a good end**

解析 make ... come to a good end意思是「讓……可以順利收場」。在商場，若不損及自身利益，紛爭能免則免。

② **truly know what sb. want**

解析 truly know what sb. want意思是「你真的了解……想

法」。就買賣雙方來看，當賣方深切了解買方的需求，就算交易過程中有摩擦，要消弭也較容易。因此，當我們在開會時要表達對與某客戶的掌握程度甚高時，就可以用 we truly know what...want, so.... 來表示。

③ **get someone's point**

解析 get someone's point 意思是「理解……的想法」。就處理客訴的角度看，若賣方或是服務提供者能夠準確理解消費者產生不滿的原因，處理的速度與效果自然快又好。

As I know, such change **results from** the budget adjustment of logistics.
就我所知，會有這樣的變化是因為物流的預算改變。

★ As I know, the budget control of logistics **is the main cause of** such change.

★ As I know, the budget control of logistics **results in** such change.

★ As I know, such change **happens because of** the budget control of logistics.

 解析時間

① **Sth. is the main cause of...**

解析 is the main cause of... 意思是「某事物是……的主因」。由於事件的發生一定有主要與次要因素，因此當在會議中要說明某因素幾乎左右某事的發生與否，就可以用 Sth. is the main cause of... 來表示。

② **result in**

解析 result in 意思是「導致」，與 result from 在概念上剛好相反。因此 A result in B= B result from A。在開會中，若要強調原因，就使用 result，若要強調結果，則用 result from。

③ **Sth. happen because of N**

解析 Sth. happen because of N 意思是「某事發生是因為……」，此用法將論述重點著放在原因，唯需特別注意其後要加上名詞而不是子句。當在你會議中有需要強調事件起因時，就可以用 Sth. happen because of N 來表示。

E 非學不可的職場小貼示

　　大家可能都知道 logistics 這個單字意思是物流，但如果問到物流概念的起源以及包含哪些面向，如果沒有具備商科背景，就不是這麼熟悉了。物流一字源於希臘語 Logistikos，意思是精於計算，是從軍事的後勤概念演變而來。一般來說，大家都會覺得物流就只包含商品的運輸與儲存，但事實上加工處理也是物流的一環，因此未來當你參與關於物流的會議時，發現有 processing（食品加工）、machining（機械、物件加工）這些面向時，就不會太訝異了。

Part 2 【內勤】辦公室會議篇

Done deal 搞定／定案

A 辭彙文化背景介紹

若要充分理解此用法的語意如何產生，需從 do deal 的字面意思看起，do 意思是「做…」，deal 意思是交意，兩者相加就是「做交易」。當交易完成了，就可以用 a done deal 表示。

理解字面後，接下來我們再就此商業行為的目地面做探討。仔細想想，做交易的最終目的是要成交，換句話說就是要搞定這筆交易。而已經成交的交易因為不得變更任何部分，代表一切已成定局。

透過上述推演過程，讓我們知道原來 do deal 的意思「是搞定…」，而 done deal 指的是「已成定局」。因此，往後如果在會議中要表達正在處理某事了，就可以用 I am doing deal with… 來表示。如果是已經處理好某事，就可用 …is a done 做說明。

B 看看辭彙怎麼用

【同事間】Between colleagues

Sophia 蘇菲亞	As the host of the **charity** baseball game in Taipei, we have to deal with the sponsorship half a year prior to the game. Next Monday is the first progress meeting, what have you done, Tom?	身為台北慈善棒球賽的主辦單位，我們必須在賽前半年搞定所有的贊助，下週一就要開第一次進度會議，湯姆你現在進度到哪邊了？
Tom 湯姆	KLO shows great interest in supporting the transportation fee of the **minority** groups to the baseball field, so I am double checking the list we would like to invite and send it to them later.	KLO對於贊助弱勢團體到場看球的交通費表達高度意願，所以我現在正在再次確認邀請名單，稍後會將名單寄給KLO。
Sophia	Drawing the lottery from all ticket buyers is the option we could consider, so I have contacted with Lance Automobile to seek for the sponsorship in the **jackpot**.	由於讓購票進場的觀眾有抽獎機會是可以考慮的方向，我已經和藍斯汽車接洽贊助大獎的相關事宜。

Part 2

【內勤】辦公室會議篇

| | Good. Since 50 percent of the ticket income will be donated, I find it necessary to create certain **incentive** to attract people to come. | 太棒了。由於百分之五十門票收入將捐做慈善用途，我覺得有必要創造誘因讓更多人進場看球。 |

| Tom | What response do you get? | 那你的回應是？ |

| Sophia | Viewing helping the minority as CSR, Lance Automobile's General Manager accepts my request without hesitation. What we have to do is to sign the related document to finish the procedure, <u>namely getting a car as the jackpot is almost a done deal</u>. | 視協助有需要的人為企業社會責任，蘭斯汽車的總經理毫不猶豫地一口答應。所以接下來我們要做的只剩簽署相關文件，等同我們幾乎已經談妥以汽車做為大獎一事。 |

【主管與屬下間】

Between the supervisor and the employee

| Julia 茱莉雅 | Morning everyone. The issue we will cover today is how to create more buzz for our product. Please feel free to express your ideas. | 各位早安。今天會議的主題是要如何替公司產品創造更多話題性，請各位暢所欲言。 |

**Emily
艾蜜莉**

According to my observation, the **texture** of clothing is not in the priority for many fashion pursuers. What they care about is how special the item is, so I think developing a series of crossover with the brand which seems no connection with us could be an option. Here I can give you all a successful case, Adida and goodtears. Adida is famous for its sports shoes, while goodtears is a tire manufacturer. The two brands are **poles apart** but rubber is the material they use **in common**. We can use this model as the origin to find out who is the suitable partner.

根據我的觀察，對追逐潮流的人來說，服飾的質料不是優先考量，他們在乎的是夠不夠特別，因此我覺得跟看起來兩者毫無關連的品牌發展聯名商品會是個不錯的想法。這邊我可以舉出一個成功的案例，就是Adida和goodtears。Adida以其運動鞋聞名，而goodtears是輪胎製造商。兩者天差地遠，但卻都使用橡膠做為原料。我們可以以此模式做為源頭，找出誰會是適合的合作夥伴。

**Lulu
露露**

I think 2Nature is the one we can take into consideration. This brand advocates eating nature and we use nature dyes. Going nature could be the feature of items we would like to release in this cooperation.

我想2Nature是我們可以考慮的對象。這間公司主打天然飲食，而我們都使用天然染記。自然取向可以是本次合作所有商品的主要特色。

| Julia | Good suggestion. Now I officially authorize you two to be in charge of this project. Once both sides are about to reach the consensus in the outline, I will ask Leo to draft the contract. <u>I hope the crossover could be the done deal as soon as possible.</u> | 很好的建議。現在我正式授權兩位負責此專案。當雙方對於合作架構快達成共識時，我就會先請里歐草擬合約。我希望此次聯名可以盡快成定局。 |

 C 對話單字、片語說分明

① **charity** *ph.* 慈善

例 This concert is held out of charity, so please come if you are free at that time.
此音樂會因慈善目的所舉辦，所以如您有空請務必共襄盛舉。

② **minority** *n.* 弱勢

例 To help the minority, we offer this group a favor price in purchasing computers as long as they show us the related certificate.
為幫助弱勢，只要出示相關證明，我們就給與購機優惠。

③ **incentive** *n.* 誘因

例 The limited free gift is the greatest incentive for consumers in this sale.

在本次特賣中，免費限量贈品最能吸引消費者。

④ **jackpot** *n.* 大獎

例 Since ABC tends to buy 1000 machines at once, getting this order is like hitting the jackpot

由於ABC公司打算一次購買1千台機器，得到這張訂單就跟中大獎沒兩樣。

⑤ **texture** *n.* 材質

例 Considering the softness in texture, we use nature rubber.

考量到材質的柔軟性，我們選用天然橡膠。

⑥ **be poles apart** *ph.* 天差地遠

例 The two companies are poles apart in business but now they form a strategic alliance.

兩間公司的性質天差地遠，但現在卻建立策略聯盟。

⑦ **in common** *ph.* 共同的

例 Provide the best service to the consumers is the faith we and our sub-brand share in common.

提供消費者最好的服務是我們與旗下副牌所共同秉持的信念。

D 換句話說補一補

Since 50 percent of the ticket income will be donated, I find it necessary to **create certain incentive** to attract people to come.

由於百分之五十門票收入將捐做慈善用途，我覺得有必要創造誘因讓更多人進場看球。

★ Since..., I find it necessary to **create more buzzes for this game**.

★ Since..., **more audience means more dotation**.

★ Since..., **the box office determines the total volume of the donation**.

 解析時間

① **create more buzzes for ...**

> **解析** create more buzzes for...意思是「為⋯⋯創造更多話題」。就行銷角度看，活動越有話題性，商機就越多，因此當開會主題有關廣告行銷時，就可以用 to create more for..., we...這類句型開頭，然後說明自己目前所規劃的內容為何。

② **more N means more N**

> **解析** more audience means more dotation意思是「越多⋯⋯等同越多⋯」。由於此用法所描述的兩個事物屬於正相關，因此當在會議中要說明提升或改善某一要素所能帶來的正面效果時，就可以用 more...means more... 來表示。

168

③ **the N1 determine the total volume of the N2**

解析 the N1 determine the total volume of the N2意 思 是
「…決定…的總量」，代表了兩個因素有正向關連。N1 提高
則N2 的總量增加，反之則為減少。因此，當要在會議中敘
述這類對應關係時，就可以the N1 determine the total
volume of the N2來表示。

Viewing helping the minority as **CSR**, Lance Automobile's
General Manager accepts my request without hesitation.
視協助有需要的人為企業社會責任，蘭斯汽車的總經理毫不猶豫地一
口答應。

★ Viewing helping the minority as **thefeedback to the
society**, Lance Automobile's General Manager...

★ Viewing helping theminority as **the obligation an
enterprise could fulfill**, Lance Automobile's General
Manager...

★ **Taking helping the minority as granted to a successful
enterprise**, Lance Automobile's General Manager...

 解析時間

① **the feedback to ....**

解析 the feedback to...意思是「對……的回饋」。在商場上，除
了追求利潤外，適度的回饋可使業務推展更順利，因此，若會
議主題是關於回饋客戶，就可以用N can be the feedback
to our clients表示。

② **the obligation a n. could fulfill**

解析 the obligation a *n.* could fulfill意思是「……所可以肩負的責任」。此用法通常用於表述企業對於社會的回饋，因此，若要表達做某件事情可以體現出「取之於社會，用之於社會」的精神時就可以用 ...is the obligation we can could fulfill to the society來表示。

③ **taking ....as granted tosb.**

解析 taking ...as granted to ...意思是「對……來說，做……實為理所當然」。此用法可用來表達企業或是員工對於某種現象或事件的看法。因此，當我們覺得以公司的現況或是地位，做某事是理所當然時，就可以用taking ...as granted to ... we should...來表示。

The two brands are **poles apart** but rubber is the martial they use in common.
兩者天差地遠，但卻都使用橡膠做為原料。

★ The two brands **are from different fields** but rubber...
★ The two brands **had no connection in essence** but rubber...

 解析時間

① **Ns are from different fields**

解析 Ns are from different fields意思「是……是來自不同領域」。若要進行商業合作，異業結盟有是可以激盪出新的火

花，因此當要在會議中強調此點時，就可以用 A and us are from different fields,so... 來表示。

② **Ns have no connection in essence**

解析 Ns have no connection in essence意思是「……在本質上沒有連結性」。如果兩個品牌本質完全不同，最後卻能結盟推出產品，必能引起消費者注意，因此若要在開會中表達從不同中找相同的思維，就可以用Ns have no connection in essence, but... 來表示。

 **E** 非學不可的職場小貼示

對話中的CSR是Corporate Social Responsibility的縮寫，意思是企業社會責任，在許多企業的章程內都有提到此部分，但其概念較接近某種道德規範或意識形態。

企業社會責任說穿了就很像是假如今天你是從某處發跡，後來賺大錢了，就應該拿一部分利潤來回饋鄉里，但如果你選擇不這樣做，也沒有法律條文會制裁你。

理解了企業社會責任後，下次如果希望公司高層批准進行公益活動，就可以用Considering the corporate social responsibility, we shall... 做為你報告的開頭語句。

Part 3
【外勤】業務／採購銷售篇

<table>
<tr><td>Unit
17</td><td>**Bait and switch**
引誘消費者購買</td></tr>
</table>

 A 辭彙文化背景介紹

　　Bait指的是「誘餌」，switch意思是「掉包」，就其字面來看就是「靠誘餌使獵物上鉤然後掉包」，是一種存心欺騙的銷售手法，但為何許多不肖商人仍能得逞呢？以下就從其字面意思一路推敲下去。

　　此種手法的「誘餌」就是「低價促銷」，由於人都會想貪小便宜，因此很容易被此類型的廣告吸引，但當他們進入店裡想選擇商品時，卻被告知該項商品已經售完，銷售員轉而向其不斷推銷高價商品，所以此處的「掉包」就是「以高價品換替低價品」，由於消費者會想趕快脫身，業者就可趁機狠敲竹槓。

　　透過上述的推演，會發現這樣的欺騙手法，很接近中文中所講的「掛羊頭，賣狗肉」，因此當未來你在進行採購時，如果發現對方不老實有高賣之嫌，就可以用Don't apply bait and switch tactics, or I will...（別想要耍什麼手段，否則……。）這類句型給予警告，以保護公司權益。

B 看看辭彙怎麼用

【同事間】 **Between colleagues**

Emma 艾瑪	Our new office in Singapore is about to open, how is the **interior** decorating, Jenny?	我們新加坡的辦公室即將啟用，目前裝潢進度如何呢？
Jenny 珍妮	Almost done. But to be honest, the purchase process is filled with twists and turns. I am so glad that I don't mess it up in the long run.	幾乎都好了。但說真的，採購過程一波三折，我很慶幸最後沒有搞砸。
Emma	Poor Jenny, what kind of troubles have you encountered?	辛苦你了，到底是碰到哪些問題呢？
Jenny	To meet the estimated budget, I found office equipment company named U-star. Its advertisement features U-236 series is on a special sales. So I contacted their factory to check whether it is worthy of buying or not. What surprises me is this series is not available for long, but U-star still uses it as the **selling point**.	為了要符合預算，我找到一間叫做U-star的辦公用品公司。該公司以U-236系列做為主打，所以我就聯絡其工廠確認是否值得採購。但令我驚訝的是這個系列早已缺貨多時，但U-star仍以此做為賣點。

Part 3

【外勤】業務／採購銷售篇

What's even worse is the sales started to recommend those high-class equipment with no discount at all. <u>Knowing that U-star tends to play the bait and switch trick, I made up an excuse and leave.</u>

更糟的是，業務開始向我推銷沒有折扣的高價設備。知道U-star想搞掛羊頭賣狗肉的把戲，我捏造了一個理由就趕緊離開。

Emma What a terrible company. Compared to U-star, BISN you choose is more **reliable**. BISN aims to provide the best arrangement for their customer, so I am truly satisfied with their service.

好糟糕的一間公司。與U-star相比，你最後選擇的BISN公司有信用多了。該公司會替客戶做最適當的安排，所以我真的對他們的服務感到滿意。

Jenny True. Honesty is the best policy. BISN treats consumers with a sincere attitude, so I cannot come up with a reason of not using their products.

沒錯，誠實才是上策。BISN真誠對待客戶，所以我想不出不選用他們產品的理由。

【主管與屬下間】

Between the supervisor and the employee

Thomas 湯瑪士	I have heard AMN Clothing has been removed from the **pocket list** of the purchase of new uniform. What's going on, Samuel? I have contacted with them for three times, so I assume AMN could win the order.	我聽說AMN服飾已經被從本次新制服採購案的口袋名單中剔除了，到底發生什麼事了，山謬？我跟AMN會面過三次，我都以為應該是他們拿到這張訂單了。
Samuel 山謬	Everything seems to go well before my last visit to their company. Regarding this deal will be done soon, I listed the size, types, and all the other details for final confirmation. But when I had a meeting with their sales who is in charge of this purchase, her answer made me shocked. She told me that she didn't know **textile** we would like to use had not been available since last month, so we had to pay more to change the material or the delivery date would be postponed.	在我最後一次去拜訪該公司前，一切看起來都沒問題。認為本次採購就快定案了，我列出尺寸、型號等細節要做最後確認。但等我與對方負責此專案的業務開會時，她卻跟說我她不知道我們要使用的布料上個月就已經缺貨了，所以我們必須加錢換布料或延後出貨。

Thomas Ridiculous. Being a sales, you have no excuse to say something like "I didn't know the raw material is out of stock." What did you do after listening to her reply?

這太荒謬了。身為業務，不可以說像是：「我不知道哪些原物料已經缺貨。」的這種話。聽完她的回覆你怎麼處理呢？

Samuel I said, "Considering the budget and the delivery date, I am sorry to say we may need to find the other company to produce the uniform for us. Hope we still have the chance to cooperate in the future." However, my true feeling in mind is that AMN Clothing meant to play the bait and switch trick, so putting this company in the **blacklist** is needed.

我說：「考量到預算以及出貨時間，這邊我很抱歉的向您表示敝公司可能要另尋其他公司製做制服，希望未來還有與您合作的機會。但我心理實際的感受是覺得AMN服飾存心玩掛羊頭賣狗肉的把戲，所以應該把它列入黑名單。

Thomas You play cards right.

你的處理很恰當。

對話單字、片語說分明

① **interior** *adj.* 內部的

例 Though this project is urgent, you still need to finish the interior procedure.

雖然此專案很緊急，但你還是得走完內部流程。

② **selling point** *n.* 賣點

例 The crossover item is our selling point of this marketing campaign.

跨界商品是本次行銷活動的賣點。

③ **make up** *v.* 捏造

例 To escape from the embarrassing situation in the meeting, I made up an excuse and left early.

為了遠離會議中的尷尬氛圍，我編造一個理由後就早退。

④ **reliable** *adj.* 值得信賴的

例 The data from this organization is reliable, so you can use it in the report without worries.

此機構的資料可信度高，所以你可以在報告中放心使用。

⑤ **pocket list** *n.* 口袋名單

例 The following is the pocket list you can consider in this project.

以下是本次專案你可以列入考慮的口袋名單。

Part 3

【外勤】業務／採購銷售篇

⑥ **textile** *n.* 布料

例 Our apparel uses top textile, so you can tell the difference easily.

我們的服飾使用頂級布料，所以你可以輕鬆感覺出差異。

⑦ **blacklist** *n.* 黑名單

例 Since this company delayed the payment all the time, we put it into our blacklist.

由於這間公司經常拖欠款項，我們將其列入黑名單。

 D 換句話說補一補

But to be honest, the purchase process is filled with **twists and turns**.

但說真的，採購過程一波三折。

★ But to be honest, **the obstacles I have faced in this purchase are difficult**.

★ But to be honest, this purchase **is no easy task**.

★ But to be honest, **it takes me great efforts to make a deal with this purchase**.

 解析時間

① **the obstacles sb. have faced in ... are difficult**

解析 the obstacles sb. have faced in ... are difficult意　思「是……在……中遇到的阻礙很困難」。當在交易過程中遇到阻礙，要耗費的心力自然也高。

② **... is no easy task**

解析 ... is no easy task意思是「……不是件簡單的工作」。在業務往來上，並非每次都一帆風順，難免有碰到棘手狀況時候，因此，若當你發現自己所負責的案子老是出問題時，就可以用 ...is no easy task來表示。

③ **it takes sb. great efforts to make a deal with this...**

解析 it takes sb. great efforts to make a deal with this...意思是「……花了很大功夫才搞定……」。此用法中的great efforts與make a deal with都表現出事情的難處理程度甚高，因此若你覺得這完全說中你手邊業務或生意的現況時，就可以用 it takes me great efforts to make a deal with this...來表示。

What surprises me is this series is not available for long, but U-star still uses it as the **selling point**.

令我驚訝的是這個系列早已缺貨多時，但U-star仍以此做為賣點。

★ What surprises me is this series is not available for long, but U-star still **features the product**.

★ What surprises me is this series is not available for long, but U-star still **hides the news**.

★ What surprises me is this series is not available for long, but U-star **means to cheat**.

Part 3 【外勤】業務／採購銷售篇

解析時間

① **feature...**

【解析】 feature... 意思是「主打……」。在銷售產品時,一定會有主打商品與非主打商品。因此,當你認為某項商品很有商機,應多加推銷時,就可以用 we should feature...because... 來表示。

② **hide this news**

【解析】 hide this news 意思是「隱藏消息」。在交易過程中,如出現不利自己的因素,買賣雙方都可能會刻意隱瞞,因此當你覺得對方似乎有在掩蓋某些訊息時,就可以用 Don't hide the news, just... 釋出要彼此坦承的訊息。

③ **mean to v.**

【解析】 mean to v. 意思是「存心…」。正所謂人心險惡,在商場上有些人就是刻意要佔人便宜,因此當你在交易或是業務往來中發現此種情況,就可以用 sb. means to..., so we... 來表達應當制止的立場。

Being a sales, you **have no excuse to say** something like "I didn't know the raw material is out of stock."
不可以說像是:「我不知道哪些原物料已經缺貨。」的這種話。

★ Being a sales, you **have the responsibility to** know which raw material is in lack.

★ Being a sales, **saying** "I didn't know the raw material is in lack." **is not accepted**.

解析時間

① **Sb.has the responsibility to...**

解析　sb.has the responsibility to... 意思是「某人有責任去……」，此用法可用於是說明某個職位的職責為何。因此，當在業務或生意往來中發現某人明顯失職，但又不想直接點破，就可以用 Sb. have the responsibility to...,so... 來表達。

② **Ving... is not accept**

解析　V.ing... is not accept 意思是「做……是不被允許的」。此用法改用排除法來說明職責，因此當在職場上發現某人做出其職位所不該或不能做的事，就可以用 Being a..., Ving... is not accepted 來表示。

 非學不可的職場小貼示

　　本單元對話中出現的 office equipment 其實就是大家所熟知的 OA，也就是辦公室用品。OA 中的 O 相信大家都知道是 office，那 A 指得是什麼呢？答案是 accessory。Accessory 指的是「配件」，辦公室裡除了基本裝潢隔間外，如果沒有這些配件根本無法辦公，因此 OA 是大家工作時所不可或缺的。但隨著科技進步，OA 現在不見得都意指 office accessory。辦公室自動化（office automation）的縮寫也是 OA，因此未來當聽到有人在討論 OA 時，記得留意一下到底在說哪一個，才不會貼笑大方喔！

Unit 18 Straight from the horse's mouth 消息來源可靠

 A 辭彙文化背景介紹

如果單看字面，straight from the horse's mouth 意思就是「直接從馬的嘴巴」。那從馬的嘴巴又能看出甚麼端倪呢？

馬嘴巴裡最多的東西就是牙齒，而且從牙齒的數量、長度、形狀等特徵，就可以算出馬的年紀。初生的小馬沒有牙齒，要等一小段時間才會乳牙，而長到成馬後再由恆齒所替代，整個生長歷程實在難以造假。

而既然看過牙齒就一定可以算出年紀，馬的牙齒後來就被借代成「斷定某事的關鍵證據」，整個慣用語也就衍生出「消息來源是準確可靠」的意思。因此未來當你獲得某項資訊後，覺得其來源可靠，希望對方可以信任你時，就可以用 I get this information straight from horse's mouth, so you can... 來表示

B 看看辭彙怎麼用

【同事間】Between colleagues

Shaw 蕭	Most of the computers we are using now can't perform well, so I think it is about time to apply for the **replacement**. Personally, I prefer Acers because it provides a two-year **warranty**. How do you feel, Jason?	目前大部分我們所使用的電腦，多數都效能不佳，所以我覺得應該申請汰換了。我個人偏好採購Acers，因為他們提供2年的保固服務。傑森你覺得呢？
Jason 傑森	In terms of free warranty, Acers do rank number one in the market. But if we put the cost-effectiveness into consideration, Usas' GT68 series is the top choice.	如果講到免費保固，Acers的確在業界榮膺第一。但如果把划算度也列入考慮，Usas的GT68系列絕對是首選。
Shaw	GT68 series is still one of the top models in the market, so I really wonder in what sense you can say it is cost effective.	GT68目前還是市場中的頂級機種之一，所以我真的很好奇你是根據那一方面來說此系列很划算。

Jason	A little bird tells me that Usas has developed a new chip, so a new series will be released next quarter. To feature the new product and clear the inventory, GT68 series will have a great discount.	據消息靈通人士指出 Usas 已經研發出新的晶片，所以下一季會推出新的系列。為了主打新商品並出清存貨。GT68 系列會有大折扣。
Shaw	Are you sure? GT68 series is **categorized** in a high-end commercial computer, so the range of the discount is relative small since its debut.	你確定？GT68 系列被歸在高階商用機種，所以從推出以來折價空間就有限。
Jason	I get this information straight from the horses' month, so you can 100 percent trust me. If I were wrong, I would treat you coffee for one week. But if I were right, you would **owe** me a fancy lunch.	我的消息來源準確無誤，所以你可以百分之百相信我。如果的消息錯誤，我請你喝咖啡一個星期，但如果消息正確，你欠我一頓豐盛的午餐。
Shaw	Come on, I am just kidding. Since you have a tip-off, I will adopt your option to save money in this purchase.	別這樣，我開玩笑的。既然你有線報，我會採用你的選擇，好在這次採購中省錢。

【主管與屬下間】

Between the supervisor and the employee

Peter 彼得	Considering the room of the official **vehicle** in service is too small, General Manager's Special Assistant has asked me to find a car around 200,000 USD. And the old one will be available for a business purpose for all the managing level. The first thought that comes into my mind is DENZ AGM636, what about you, Mark?	考量到舊的公務車空間太小，總經理特助要我去找一台大約20萬美金左右的新車。而原來的公務車就開放給所有管理階層做公務用途使用。我第一個想到的車款就是DENZ的AGM636，馬克你覺得呢？
Mark 馬克	A GM636 is a good choice, but I don't suggest you buy it at this moment.	AGM636是很棒的選擇，但此時我建議不要買這款車。
Peter	What do you mean by saying this?	你這樣說的意思是？

Part 3

【外勤】業務／採購銷售篇

187

Mark	DENZ would have upgraded in this model soon. <u>I get this news straight from horse's mouth, so you can put my opinion into consideration.</u> The upgraded model is called AGM638. AGM638 and AGM636 only have 3000 USD differences in price, but the **performance** is better. And more importantly, the room is bigger.	DENZ車場針對此車款即將有改款。我的消息來源絕對正確，所以你可把我的意見納入考量。升級款叫做AGM638。AGM638只比AGM636貴3千美金，不但效能更好，更重要的是空間更大。
Peter	Since you have received the insider's suggestion, let's wait a moment until AGM638 is **released**. I will convey this message to special assistant. Good job, Mark.	既然你已得到知情人士的建議，我們就等到AGM638上市再買車。我會把此訊息告知特助。馬克，做得好。

C 對話單字、片語說分明

① **replacement** *n.* 汰換

例 This machine has reached its product life cycle, so it is time for the replacement.

這台機器已達使用年限，所以是時候汰換了。

② **warranty** *n.* 保固

例 The warranty will come into effect right after your purchase.

保固於購買後立即生效。

③ **categorized** *v.* 分類

例 Equipped with the latest chip, the computer is categorized in the high end series.

由於配有最新型晶片，此電腦被歸類為高階機種。

④ **owe** *v.* 虧欠

例 I will definitely in a big trouble without your help in this project, so I owe you one favor.

此專案如果沒有你的幫忙我肯定會出大包，所以我欠你一份人情。

⑤ **vehicle** *n.* 交通工具

例 Considering the expense in vehicle, we provide you a 10 USD subsidy.

考量到交通費，我們提供你10美金的資費補貼。

⑥ **performance** *n.* 效能

例 To improve the performance, a new chip is equipped with in this smartphone.

為增進效能，這款手機搭載新款晶片。

Part 3

【外勤】業務／採購銷售篇

⑦ **release** *v.* 上市

 This phone is scheduled to be released this May.
此款手機預計今年五月上市。

D 換句話說補一補

But if we take the cost-effectiveness into consideration, Usas' GT68 series is the **top choice**.
但如果把划算度也列入考慮，Usua的GT68系列絕對是首選。

★ But if we take the cost-effectiveness into consideration, Usas' GT68 series **is the item you can't miss**.

★ But if we take the cost-effectiveness into consideration, Usas' GT68 series **is the most recommended**.

 解析時間

① **the item sb. can't miss**

解析 the item sb. can't miss意思是「……不能錯過的品項」。當有人告訴你某產品不容錯過，代表此產品要不就是很划算，不然就是完全符合你的要求。因此，未來在購買物品時，不論你是給別人建議，或是請別人給你建議，都可以用...is the item sb. can't miss來表示。

② **...is the most recommended**

解析 the most recommended意思是「最推薦的……」。當某項產品被列為最推薦，代表該產品的某項特性（價格、功能等）為多數人接受。因此，當你購買產品時選擇相信大家的推薦，就可以用在According to the..., ...is the most recommended 來表示。

Since you have **a tip-off**, I will adopt your option to save money in this purchase.
既然你有線報，我會採用你的選擇，好在這此採購中省錢。

★ Since you **have received a reminder**, I will...
★ Since you **have gotten the information from the insider**, I will...
★ Since you **have disclosed the unrevealed information**, I will...

 解析時間

① **have received a reminder**

解析 have received a reminder意思是「已經得到提示」。如在購買產品前已經收到風聲將有漲跌或是改款，就可做出最適當的對應措施。因此，當你有這樣的管道時，就可以用I have received a reminderabout...., so...來提醒同事應及早或稍後再購買。

② **get the information from...**

解析 get the information from...意思是「從……獲得資訊」。在

Part 3

【外勤】業務／採購銷售篇

本例句中的insider指的是知道內情人士，但畢竟不是每個人在採購時都有此管道，因此只要是從某人那邊獲得消費資訊，就可以用 I get the information from...,so I... 來表示。

③ **Sb. has disclosed the unrevealed information**

(解析) sb. has disclosed the unrevealed information意思是「某人已經揭露未公開訊息」。此用法在概念上就是根據線報指出某事即將發生，因此當我們從某人那邊得知小道消息，知道接下來應該怎樣消費最划算，就可以用 Since sb. has disclosed the unrevealed information, I.... 來表示。

And the old one will **be available for** a business purpose for all the managing level.
而原來的公務車就開放給所有管理階層做公務用途使用。

★ And all the managing level **has the right to use** the old car for a business purpose.
★ And the old one will **be open for** a business purpose for all the managing level.
★ And the old one can **serve as the official vehicle** for all the managing level.

 解析時間

① **have the right to v.**

(解析) have the right to v. 意思是「有權利做……」。在採購過程中，除非是最高主管，否則你無法決定所有事情。因此，

如果在請示過後獲得長官授權，就可以用Receiving the authorization/permission from..., now I have the right to...來表示。

② **be open for**

解析 be open for意思是「開放給……」。與上述用法相同，本用法也是在強調權限的開放，但差別在於本用法是從管理階層的角度看。因此，當長官願意開放某些權限給下屬，就可以用...is open for...來表示。

③ **serve as the n.**

解析 serve as the N.意思是「做為……」。此用法經常用於描述某項事物功用的改變。因此當你要表達這樣的變化時，就可以用N. used to be the...of ..., but now it serve as...N.來表示。

E 非學不可的職場小貼示

　　對話中所出現debut一字其實指的是演員的初登場。此單字並非英文，而是法文，但已經為英語使用者所習慣。現在舉凡新產品發表或企業新官上任，都有人以此單字表示。下次當要表達產品的發行或是人物的登場，你腦袋中就不會只有release、show up這幾個單字，會知道debut可以簡潔有力的表達「首次出現」的意思。

Unit 19 Test the water 試水溫

A 辭彙文化背景介紹

從字面看，test the water意思就是「測試水的某種特性」。雖然可測試的項目多到難以細數，但很多需要借助科學儀器，才能獲得一個絕對值。雖然水溫也是個測定值，但每個人最喜歡的溫度，就沒有一個固定值。

若要找出自己最喜歡的水溫，最簡單的方式就是把手指頭放進水裡，實際感受溫度。由於在受測前完全不知道溫度，所以當下的反應是最準確的。無獨有偶地，商品行銷事前會先進行分析，然後得出某項結果，但測試結果是否會真如預期，還是要實際操作過才知道。

由於測水溫與市場行銷在概念上有諸多相似性，因此我們現在早已把試水溫直接作為新品行銷的代名詞。廠商會根據市場反應來修正路線與產品，已達最佳銷售情況。因此，未來公司推出新產品，而你剛好負責測試市場反應，就可以用I am testing the water來表示。

看看辭彙怎麼用

【同事間】Between colleagues

Harden
哈登

Noticing the great growth in the night running **population**, I think it is a good time to combine technology with sports. The prototype in my mind is called e-jacket.

眼見夜跑的人口越來越多，我覺得現在是個結合科技與運動的好時機。我腦中的現有雛型叫做e-外套。

(continued)

（繼續解釋）

Harden

Living in an information era, most runners will use their mobile phone while running. However, listening to music and recording the data may consume great power, making necessary to find a way to **recharge**. Though a power bank seems to be the panacea for this, but it is really **annoying** for runners. To solve the two problems at once, the idea of recharging while running sounds excellent. And that is the feature of our e-jacket.

生活在資訊世代，多數跑者跑步時都會使用手機。但是聽音樂跟紀錄資訊可能會消耗不少電力，因此就充電的必要。雖然帶顆行動電源好像就解決所有問題了，但這對跑者來說何其麻煩。為了要同時解決上述的問題，邊跑就邊充電的想法感覺很棒。而這也是這件e外套的最大特色。

Derrick 德瑞克	A practical idea, but can you explain it to me as to why you'd like to apply the theory in it.	非常實際的想法，但可以跟我解釋一下你所想應用在其中的原理嗎？
Harden	Sure. I will put a small generator inside the sleeve of jacket, and the movement while running will be **transformed** into electricity. Once the runner uses cables to connect his or her phone with the generator, recharging is ready to begin.	當然可以。我會在外套袖子裡放一個小發電機，跑步時的動作會被轉換成電力。一旦跑者用充電線連接發電機，充電便準備就緒。
Derrick	I see. In that sense, I think it is worthy trying. After testing the water, we will know whether your idea is a great hit or a total failure in the market.	我了解了。如果是這樣的產品，我覺得值得一試。測過市場水溫後。我們就會知道你的想法是一舉成名還是一敗塗地了。

【主管與屬下間】

Between the supervisor and the employee

Ashley
艾希禮

As we know, the **cutting-throat** competition in clothing industry constrains the profit. Though cheap price is a strong incentive, more and more consumers care creativity more because they want to be unique. And that is the reason why I gather you all to have a discussion concerning the new ideas in design. Express yourself, please.

相信大家都知道，服飾業的割喉競爭壓縮了利潤。雖然低價是個很強的誘因，但越來越多消費者重視創意，因為他們想要讓自己看起來特別。而這也是今天我招集各位來討論新設計的原因。請大家暢所欲言。

Mandy
蔓蒂

The Chinese style has been popular for a long time, so I think they can be the main spirit of the new series.

中國風一直以來都很流行，所以我覺得可以以此做為新系列的設計精神所在。

Daisy

Your words inspire me. A Chinese cotton padded jacket is classic winter wearing, but the young generation views it a symbol of old school. I think we can **overturn** this **stereotype** as long as some new elements are added inside.

你的話啟發了我。中式棉襖是一款經典的冬日穿著，但年輕世代覺得它是老派的象徵。我覺得只要加入一些新元素，就可以翻轉此刻板印象。

Part 3

【外勤】業務／採購銷售篇

Mandy	The mixture of two or more materials can be considered. For example, you can use leather in sleeve, while the rest are all cotton. Or you can create a conflict feeling in the design like the Chinese style cutting with western totems.	兩種或兩種以上的材質混搭可以列入考慮，例如袖子用皮革，但其他的部分全用棉。又或是你可以創造衝突感，像是中式剪裁但加入西方圖騰。
Ashley	Your ideas seem workable, so please finish the few prototypes within two weeks. <u>Then, I will put them in our retail store for the article of the exhibition to test the water.</u>	你們的想法似乎都可行，所以請在兩周內完成一些樣板衣，我要把這些衣服拿到各分店作展示品來測測水溫。

Ⓒ 對話單字、片語說分明

① **population** *ph.* 人口

> 例 Noticing the growth in the camping population, we should release a camping car soon.
>
> 發現到露營人口正在增長，我們應當盡快推出露營車車款。

② **recharge** *v.* 充電

例 The volume of our power bank is big enough to recharge two phones at once.

我們的行動電源容量夠一次充飽兩台手機。

③ **annoying** *adj.* 惱人的

例 Though data back-up is somehow, we should do it periodically in case the unexpected system crash damage them all.

雖然資料備份有點麻煩，但我們仍應定期執行以防系統突然故障造成資料全部毀損。

④ **transform** *v.* 轉換

例 Without this adaptor, you can transform the voltage to the range which your phone and pad can use.

使用此變壓器後，你就可以將電壓轉換到你手機與平板所可使用的範圍。

⑤ **cutting-throat** adj. 割喉的

例 The cutting throat competition forces us to retreat from this market.

割喉競爭迫使我們退出此市場。

⑥ **overturn** *v.* 翻轉

例 To overturn the image of our brand, we should release some fashion items.

為了翻轉品牌形象，我們應當推出潮流產品。

⑦ **stereotype** n. 刻版印象

例 We have the stereotype that a compound material is expensive.

我們對複合材料的刻板印象就是覺得它會很貴。

 D 換句話說補一補

Noticing **the great growth in the night running population**, I think it is a good time to combine technology with sports.

眼見夜跑的人口越來越多，我覺得現在是個結合科技與運動的好時機。

★ Noticing **night running has become popular**, I think it is a good time to combine technology with sports.

★ Noticing **night running is a booming sport**, I think it is a good time to combine technology with sports.

★ Noticing night running is **a sport for all**, I think it is a good time to combine technology with sports.

 解析時間

① **N. has/have become popular**

解析 N. has/have become popular 意思是「……變得流行」。當某項產品廣為消費者接受，或是某項活動參與程度熱烈，都代表其流行度高。因此，當你發現上述情形，就可以用 N has/have become popular 來表示。

② **N. is a booming...**

〔解析〕 N. is a booming ... 意思是「N.是一項正在發展的……」。當某項活動具有發展性，代表其流行度也在提高。因此，當你覺得某項活動正在蓬勃發展，公司應當推出對應的商品，就可以用 N. is a booming... , so we should... 來表示。

After testing the water, we will know whether your idea is **a great hit or a total failure in the market.**

測過市場水溫後 我們就會知道你的想法是一舉成名還是一敗塗地了。

★ After testing the water, we will know whether **your idea is accepted or declined.**

★ After testing the water, we will know whether consumers **take it or not.**

 解析時間

① **N. is accepted or declined**

〔解析〕 N. is accepted or declined 意思是「……是被接受還是被拒絕」。就銷售來看，消費者接受代表產品有符合其需求，反之則沒有滿足要求。因此，當你想要表達某活動或是產品是否符合市場期待時，就可以用 After testing the water, we will know *n.* is accepted or declined 來表示。

② **Whether N. take it or not**

〔解析〕 whether N. take it or not 意思是「是否買帳」。就銷售來看，消費者的接受程度左右最後的業績，因此當你在執行業務或銷售上想進行某項嘗試，但不確定對方或是消費者是否接

受，就可以用 I would like to... but I don't know whether *n.* take it or not 來表示。

I think we can **overturn this stereotype** as long as some new elements are added inside.
我覺得只要加入一些新元素，就可以翻轉此刻板印象。
★ I think we can **give it a new face** as long as...
★ I think we can **surprise consumers** as long as...
★ I think we can **lead a new fashion in jacket** as long as...

 解析時間

① **give N.a new face**
> 解析　giveN.a new face 意思是「賦予……新生」。當產品有了新風貌，消費者可能就會因為新奇感而產生購買慾望，因此當你想要強調此種變化所能帶來的效益，就可以用 we can give a new face as long as... 來表示。

② **surprise...**
> 解析　surprise... 意思是「令……驚艷」。當消費者對產品感到驚艷，代表該產品有他／她所沒預期到的特色。因此當你覺得產品的某種改變可以有此效果，就可以用 With..., we can surprise... 來表示。

③ **lead a new fashion in ...**

解析 lead a new fashion in...意思是「在……引領新風潮」。當
某項產品或概念領先業界,自然會帶起一股模仿的風潮。因此
當你覺得公司的產品或是自己的想法出類拔萃,會讓人想模
仿,就可以用 ...can lead a fashion in... 來表示。

 E 非學不可的職場小貼示

　　對話中出現的 cut-throat,意思是「割喉」。若光從字
面看,感覺此用法比較像是一種戰技,而不是商業英文會出
現的用語。但如果仔細推敲文意,其實 cutting throat 用來
形容商業競爭再恰當不過了。

　　若從割喉所產生的後果來看,被攻擊的一方很可能會因
為失血過多而亡。同樣地,商場上如果被競爭對手擊潰,就
可能從此一敗塗地。由於兩者都呈現損傷一次即有可能無法
復原,因此現在大家對於 cut throat competition 這樣的
用法習以為常了。因此,下次在看到 cut-throat 一字,別
再覺得它只跟戰爭片或恐怖片有關。用來形容競爭激烈,它
是很棒的一個形容詞。

Part 3

【外勤】業務╱採購銷售篇

Cutting edge 最先進的

A 辭彙文化背景介紹

Cutting 指的是用刀之類的利器來切割東西，而 edge 意指某樣東西的邊緣。所以直觀的兩者語意相加，就是利器的鋒利邊緣，換個大家習慣的稱呼，叫做刀口。那刀口又是怎樣跟「最先進」扯上關係的呢？

最早將 cutting edge 解釋為最先進的產業是科技業，產生此用法的原因是因為刀鋒位在利器的最前端，會最先接觸到要被切割的物體。在講求不斷突破的科技業，一直處於業界的最前端，就能鞏固其領導地位。因為兩者存有這樣的相似性，後來 cutting edge 就變成形容頂尖先進技術最佳的用語。

而隨著時間演進，現在 cutting edge 已可用來泛指各行各業的頂尖技術。因此未來只要你想表達這是一項先進的技術或是產品就可以用 ... is on the cutting edge of... 來表示。

B 看看辭彙怎麼用

【同事間】Between colleagues

Russell 羅素	Next week I will have a product **presentation** to a potential buyer, can you do me a favor now?	下週我要向一位潛在客戶做產品簡報。你現在可以幫我一個忙嗎？
Bill 比爾	Sure. Want me to check whether your introduction before the operation is ok or not, right?	當然可以。是要我幫你確認操作前的介紹內容是否恰當嗎？
Russell	Yeah. Now let me begin. "Morning James. I am Russell, the sales representative of ABC Company. Thank you for sparing your precious time. The software I will **demonstrate** is our latest version of big data processing software R2Fast. Since the big data era is coming, being well-prepared in advance is a must for a successful company like yours. Optimizing the data accessing and filtering, this software is definitely the cutting edge in the market now."	沒錯。我現在就開始講：「早安，詹姆士先生。我是羅素，ABC公司的業務，今天很感謝您撥空。我所要展示的軟體是本公司最新的大數據處理軟體R2Fast。由於大數據時代已經來臨，像您這樣成功的公司更應當提早做好準備。由於在資料接受與過濾上已達最優化，這套軟體絕對是目前業界最先進的。」

Bill	90 percent is perfect, but I think you should have more background description concerning the buyer. By doing so, you can give the buyer the feeling that you have done some homework rather than having spoke out some meaningless social words.	百分之九十都很好。但我覺得你應該再增加買家的背景介紹。這樣做的話，他會覺得你有事先做功課，而不是講那種無意義應酬語。
Russell	Thank you Bill. I will cross the reference to **enhance** the content. To my appreciation, let me treat you the lunch today.	謝謝你，比爾。我會再比對資料以便增加內容。為了表達感激之意，中午我請你吃飯。
Bill	OK! Thank you, Russell.	好，那就謝謝你了，羅素。

【主管與屬下間】

Between the supervisor and the employee

| Alice 艾莉絲 | One of our main competitors released the new compression tights last week and it somehow hit the market, so can you briefly analyze the pros and cons of our product? | 我們主要的競爭對手之一上週推出一款新的壓縮褲，而且似乎轟動市場，所以可以簡單跟我分析一下公司產品的優缺點嗎？ |

Michelle 蜜雪兒	Sure. In terms of price alone, we may not have much competiveness because we feature advance sports lover. The price of our tight is much higher than that of the beginner level. <u>But if we put the technology input into consideration, our tights is undoubtedly the cutting edge in the market.</u>For most compression tights, the tightness will be affected by fiber softener. To make the cleaning of tights more simple, we develop a special fiber to solve this problem. The structure can malfunction the softener, expanding the **durability** of the tights. This technology is **the state of the art** in sports apparel, and that is the reason why we are the most beloved brand of professional athletes.

當然可以。如果單看價格，我們不太有競爭力，因為我們主打進階運動愛好者，因此在價格上比入門款貴很多。但如果把所使用科技納入考量，我們的產品絕對是業界最先進的。多數的壓縮褲，緊度都會受到柔軟精的影響。為了讓清洗壓縮褲更加簡單，我們研發一種特殊纖維。此纖維的結構可以讓柔軟精失效，延長壓縮褲的使用年限。此項科技絕對是目前市售運動服飾中最頂尖的，而這也是為何我們深受專業運動員喜愛的原因。

Alice	Since our product is highly **recognized** by so many consumers, we should keep going to make it better and better. Thank you for the presentation, Michelle.	既然我們的產品獲得許多消費者的高度認可，我們應當持續邁進，精益求精。感謝你的簡報，蜜雪兒。
Michelle	You are welcome.	不客氣。

 對話單字、片語說分明

① **presentation** *n.* 簡報

例 Thank you for sparing time from your tight schedule to hear my presentation.

感謝您百忙之中抽空聽我簡報。

② **demonstrate** *v.* 展示、示範說明

例 The machine I would like to demonstrate now is type TC-1875.

我現在要展示的機器是TC-1875型。

③ **filter** *v.* 過濾

例 To filter the unnecessary data, the software will categorize information by some key words.

為了過濾掉無用的資料，此軟體會按照某些關鍵字分類資訊。

④ **enhance** *v.* 改善

例 The modification is to enhance the proficiency in data accessing.

此修正就是為了改善資料獲取速度。

⑤ **durability** *n.* 耐用度

例 This machine is famous for its durability.

此機器以耐用出名。

⑥ **the state of the art** *ph.* 最先進的

例 In terms of audio visual effect, this TV is the state of the art.

就影音效果來看，這台電視是最先進的。

⑦ **recognize** *v.* 認可

例 Since this marketing model has been recognized by the managing level, we can initiate it from the next quarter.

由於此行銷模式已獲得管理階層的認可，下一季起即可開始執行。

Optimizing the data accessing and Filtering, this software is definitely **the cutting edge in the market**.

由於在資料接受與過濾上已達最優化，這套軟體絕對是目前業界最先進的。

★ Optimizing the data accessing and Filtering, this software is definitely the **bellwether** in the market.

★ Optimizing the data accessing and Filtering, this software is definitely **the state of the art** in the market.

 解析時間

① **bellwether**

解析 bellwether意思是「領頭羊」。由於羊群會跟隨帶頭的那隻羊來進行移動，因此領頭羊也可用來指稱具領導地位。因此，若要強調產品或是技術是同行所不及，就可以用...is the bellwether in/among.... 來表示。

② **the state of the art**

解析 the state of the art意思是「最先進的」。此用法跟專利關係密切，原因在於最新的技術或產品才有可能在有人模仿之前，申請專利成功。因此，後來就也可解釋做「最先進的」。當你要表達某項產品或技術目前尚無法被模仿，就可以用...is the state of the art in... 來表示。

By doing so, you can give the buyer the feeling that you **have done some homework** rather than having spoke out some meaningless social words.

這樣做的話，他會覺得你有事先做功課，而不是講那種無意義應酬語。

★ By doing so, you can give the buyer the feeling that you **truly know what he or she may need** rather than...

★ By doing so, you can give the buyer the feeling that you **stand in my shoes** rather than...

 解析時間

① **truly know what sb. need**

〔解析〕 truly know what sb. need意思是「真的知道我可能要什麼」。就銷售的角度看，當買方覺得賣方很能理解自己的需求，做成這筆交易的機會自然就高。因此，當你做為買方，覺得對方很理解你的需求時，就可以用You truly knowwhat may I need來表示。

② **stand in one's shoes**

〔解析〕 stand in one's shoes意思是「從……的立場看」。就銷售心理學的角度看，如果賣方從買方的思考邏輯來推銷，買方接受推銷的機會相對較高。因此，當你在推銷商品時，若要表現出我是為你著想的感覺，就可以用I stand in your shoes to...來表示。

Since our product **is highly recognized by so many consumers**, we should keep going to make it better and better.

既然我們的產品獲得許多消費者的高度認可，我們應當持續邁進，精益求精。

★ Since our product **wins the recognition from consumers**, we should keep going to make it better and better.

★ Since our product **has fulfilled many consumers' need**, we should keep going to make it better and better.

★ Since **consumers have confidence in** our product, we should keep going to make it better and better.

 解析時間

① **...win the recognition from consumers**

　解析　...win the recognition from ....意思是「……贏得……的信任」。當產品或是技術獲得認可，銷售起來就相對容易。因此，當你想透過既有客群的認可，向新的客戶推銷產品時，就可以用...has win the recognition from..., so you can...來表示。

② **has fulfilled one's need**

　解析　has fulfilled one's need意思是「已經滿足……的需求」。當商品可以滿足消費者需求，獲得認同的機會自然高。因此，當你想表達公司某項產品已深獲消費者認可，所以更應當背負這些期待繼續努力時，就可以用... has fulfilled one's need, so we should...來表示。

③ **... have confidence in ...**

 ... have confidence in... 意思是「……對……有信心」。當消費者對於產品有信心，換個角度看，也就是認可這項商品。因此，當你想表達某項技術或產品已經為消費者所廣泛接受時，就可以用 have confidence in ... 來表示。

E 非學不可的職場小貼示

　　本單元中所提到 big data 指的是大數據，又可稱作 mega data，意思是規模大到無法以人工方式在合理期間內處理成適合閱讀的資料。這樣的資料隨著科技的進步，數量可能會越來越多。

　　或許我們會覺得自己好像跟這些大數據沒有關聯，但事實上大家習以為常社群網站就是有必要進行大數據分析的推手之一，透過分析當中的資料，就有機會一窺一個人的偏好，因此大數據在未來會是行銷的重要參考資料。

　　經過上述的簡單介紹，下次再看到 big data 這個單字時，你就不會覺得這個字離你好遠，而是與你工作可能息息相關了。

Cost someone an arm and a leg 荷包大失血

Unit 21

A 辭彙文化背景介紹

但就字面來看，cost someone an arm and a leg 意思是要「價值某人的一條腿與一隻手」。這樣意涵不免讓我們將此用法與野蠻做連結，想到古早以前那種「血債血還」的概念，但事實上此說法的緣起目前尚無定論，廣為使用的原因是可達誇張之效。

仔細想想，東西再貴，只要湊的出錢就還是能買到。但如果某樣東西是要你失去一隻手跟一隻腳才能得到，這樣的代價何其高昂，因為少了一隻手與腳，不死也去掉半條命。著眼於此種損失的嚴重性，後來cost someone an arm and a leg 就衍生出所費不貲的意思。

理解這層意涵後，往後當你想要表達某次的採購、維修等等情況需支付高額費用，且這樣總額會對自己或是公司財務產生明顯影響，就可以用 ...cost me/our company an arm and a lag 來表示。

B　看看辭彙怎麼用

【同事間】Between colleagues

Alex 艾力克斯	The deal with PYD Industry really lets me learn a lesson of the importance of being **detail-oriented** all the time.	與PYD工業的交易真的讓我體會到隨時保持細心的重要性。
George 喬治	What's going on? You never mentioned it before.	怎麼了？你之前從沒提起過這件事。
Alex	It is about sending a replacement. Last month PYD found the tool of one of our CNC machines has been almost **worn-out**, so they wanted me to send a new set by express. They would pay upon receiving. According to the standard operation procedure, I should have looked up our ERP system to find the exact **sequence** number.	是有關於寄送替換品。上個月PYD發現跟在我們購買的CNC機器中，有一台的刀具已經磨損得差不多了，所以他們要我以快遞寄送新的套組，貨到付款。

Part 3 【外勤】業務／採購銷售篇

At that moment, I thought it was too **troublesome** to do so because PYD order the same type for long. As a result, I omitted this step and send the tool. But very unfortunately, the tool needed that time was the only customized set they ordered. To make up this mistake, I had to cover the freight of returning and correcting item. The total is 500 USD; this amount really costs me an arm and a leg.

根據標準程序，我應該進入進銷存系統查詢確切的產品序號，但因為PYD每次都訂購相同機型，當時我覺得這樣做太麻煩了，就省去查詢的步驟直接出貨。但很不幸地，這次要換刀具的機器是唯一一組使用客製化組件那台。為了要彌補此錯誤，我得負擔退貨以及寄出正確品項所需的運費。這總共要500美金，我的荷包真的大失血。

George Poor you. I think you won't miss the checking procedure ever since.

真的苦了你了。我想自從這次有教訓後，你現在絕對不會省略檢查這個步驟了

Alex Yeah. Now I can't afford repeating the same mistakes.

是啊！再出包一次我會破產的。

【主管與屬下間】

Between the supervisor and the employee

Peter 彼得	After finding the flaw in the main parts of our machine, how's the progress in the **recall**?	自上個月發現機器主要零件有瑕疵後，目前召回的進度如何？
David 大衛	90 percent of the defective machines have been collected, while the rest 10 percent will arrive the port within one week. Since engineers all have been requested to support this special task, the replacement is scheduled to be done within 2 to 3 weeks.	百分之九十的問題機器都已回收，剩下的百分之十也將於一週內到港。由於所有工程師都被要求支援此特別業務，因此整個替換作業預計在2到3週內完成。
Peter	Good. Have the accounting department estimated expense?	很好。那會計部有估算出花費了嗎？
David	Combing the freight, the cost of part, manpower and so on, the total could reach 30,000 USD at least. This extra **expenditure diluted** the profit we have made in the last two months, so the overall performance this quarter won't be as good as we expected.	如果把運費、零件成本、人力等因素都算進去，總額最少3萬美金。此項額外支出稀釋了前兩個月的獲利，所以本季的整體表現將無法如預期般好。

| Peter | True. <u>Though the recall costs our company an arm and a leg, the business reputation we have established outweighs such expense.</u> We should solve this problem at any cost. | 沒錯。雖然召回的所費不貲，但公司所建立的信譽重於一切。所以我們應當不惜任何代價解決問題。 |
| David | You are right. Although we lose much money in the case, we win the trust and confidence from our customers by in-time risk management. | 沒錯。雖然這次我們損失不少錢，但卻以即時危機處理贏得顧客的信任與信心。 |

 C 對話單字、片語說分明

① **detail-oriented** *adj.* 細節導向

例 Being detail-oriented, Tom checks the address before shipment.

凡事都留意細節，湯姆出貨前又在檢查了一遍地址。

② **worn-out** *adj.* 用壞的

例 You have to replace the worn-out part, or the machine will be damaged.

你必須更換壞掉的零件，否則機器會損壞。

③ **sequence** *n.* 次序

例 Please check the sequence number and then ship it to Ben.

請在確認序號後將其寄給班。

④ **troublesome** *adj.* 令人煩惱的

例 It is really troublesome to align the parameter, but I have to do it every month to make sure the system is not out of order.

雖然校正參數很惱人,但我每個月還是得做一次以免系統出現故障。

⑤ **recall** *n.* 召回

例 Finding a serious design flaw, ABC Company recalled all the new product they just release.

發現設計上有重大瑕疵,ABC公司召回所有剛上市的新品。

⑥ **expenditure** *n.* 花費

例 Considering the possible expenditure is higher than we expected, we have no choice but to give up this program.

考量到花費可能比預期的還高很多,我們只好忍痛放棄此計畫。

⑦ **dilute** *v.* 稀釋

例 The high cost in raw material dilutes the profit.

原物料的高成本稀釋了獲利。

D 換句話說補一補

Last month PYD found the tool of one of our CNC machines has been almost **worn-out,** so they wanted me to send a new set by express.

上個月PYD發現跟在我們購買的CNC機器中，有一台的刀具已經磨損得差不多了。

★ Last month PYD found the tool of one of our CNC machine **should be replaced**, so they want me to send a new set by express.

★ Last month PYD **expressed the need for a tool replacement** of one of our CNC machines, so they want me to send a new set by express.

★ Last month PYD found **it is about time to replace** the tool of one of our CNC machines, so they want me to send a new set by express.

 解析時間

① **...should be replaced**

 ...should be replace意思是「……應當被更換了」。當零件或是整個產品已經使用到出現嚴重耗損，為維持正常運作，通常會建議替換新品。因此當產品售出一段時間，你想提醒客戶應當汰換部分物件時，就可以用...should be replaced when you...來表示。

② **Sb. expressed the need for...**

解析 Sb. expressed the need for...意思是「某人表達……的需求」。站在買賣的角度，如果客戶已表達某項需求，如無不太合理之處，賣方應當盡快滿足其需求。因此，當你想表達客戶已提出某項需求，且你也做好對應的準備時，就可以用Sb. expressed the need for..., so I...來表示。

③ **it is about time to replace...**

解析 it is about time to replace...意思是「是時候更換……了」。產品用久了都難免耗損，適時替換零件可延長其使用年限。

To make up this mistake, I had to cover the freight of returning and correcting items.

為了要彌補此錯誤，我得負擔退貨以及寄出正確品項所需的運費。

★ **To remedy this mistake**, I had to cover...

★ **Paying the price of this mistake**, I have to cover...

★ **To take responsibility for my carelessness**, I have to cover...

 解析時間

① **to remedy...**

解析 To remedy...意思是「為了彌補……」。人非聖賢孰能勿過，人在工作時難免有出錯的時候，只要趕快想辦法彌補，傷害就能降低。因此，當我們要替自己的錯誤善後時，就可以To remedy the... I have..., I...來表示。

② **paying the price of...**

> **解析** paying the price of ...意思是「為⋯⋯付出代價」。在工作時如果出包，通常都要花比原來更多的心力才能彌補回來，因此當你想表達這種已在承擔後果的感覺，就可以Paying the price of..., now I have to... 來表示。

③ **To take responsibility for...**

> **解析** To take responsibility for...「為⋯負起責任」。在職場上，出錯了不見得會有人幫你收拾爛攤子，自己著手處理是最保險的方法。因此，當你想呈現這種一肩扛起的感覺，就可以用To take the responsibility for ..., I... 來表示。

This extra expenditure **diluted the profit** we have made in the last two months, so the overall performance this quarter won't be as good as we expected.
此項額外支出稀釋了前兩個月的獲利，所以本季的整體表現將無法如預期般好。

★ **The profit we have made in the last two months is barely enough to pay this extra expenditure**, so...

★ This extra expenditure **made the hard working in the last two months a Sisyphus task**, so...

 解析時間

① **The... is barely enough to ....**

> **解析** The... is barely enough to ....意思是「⋯⋯只剛剛好

夠…」。若以此用法來說明損失的嚴重程度，可強調這樣的損失足以動搖過去所建立或獲得的一些事物，未來絕對不可以再犯。

② **... make the N a Sisyphus task**

解析 ....make the N a Sisyphus task 意思是「……使……像在做白工」。Sisyphus 是一位國王，他被神懲罰推石頭上山，但只要石頭接近山頂就會在自動滾下，永不終止，因此後來 Sisyphus task 指的就是做白工。當你發現有某項工作怎麼做好像都無法有太多進展，就可以用 ... make the *n.* a Sisyphus task 來表示。

 E 非學不可的職場小貼示

對話中的 recall 一字，指的就是偶爾會聽到的「召回」。在商用對話中，使用此字的機會並沒有很多，但一用到時就代表某項產品嚴重出錯，無法但靠更換或是其他方法解決問題。就使用此字頻率的高低來看，電子科技業、交通工具製造商等較有機會用到該字，而且一旦用上時，通常也是其事業危機。因此對於 recall 這個單字，我們最好就止於知道其語意，而不是真的使其發生在我們所任職的企業上。

Unit 22 Force one's hand
迫使某人提前做某事

A 辭彙文化背景介紹

雖然此用法中出現 hand 這個單字，但如果真的直譯，意思就會變成讓人一頭霧水的「脅迫某人的手」。那如果這邊 hand 意思不是「手」，指的又會是什麼呢？

此用法的源起據說跟撲克牌有關，原因在於尚未出牌前，會將牌拿在手上，所以這邊的 hand 指的就是「手中的牌」，整體的語意是「迫使某人出牌」。打牌的人都知道，會留起來的牌通常都是好牌，等到適當時機才出，所以當你有辦法逼對手提前出好牌，代表你已掌握了情勢。反之則代表你被逼到退無可退，只好出招以免輸掉牌局，此用法也因此衍生出「迫使某人提前做某事」的意涵。

當你理解這層語意，往後如果想表達自己搞定了挑剔的客戶，讓他乖乖買產品，就可以用 ...try not to..., but I force his/her hand 來表示。如果是你居於下風，則可使用 I am really reluctantto..., but... force my hand。

B 看看辭彙怎麼用

【同事間】Between colleagues

Josh
喬許

Have you **convinced** the GIO Corporation to place an order for our latest software?

你有說服GIO下單購買公司最新軟體了嗎？

Kenny
肯尼

Yes, but it is really a tough task. Since GIO just bought our software last year, they think an upgrade version is not a necessity at present. With this **premise**, they show no interest in my recommendation at the beginning.

有，但花了很大功夫。因為去年GIO才剛購買軟體，所以他們升級版並非當前所必須。在此前提下，他們一開始對我的推薦興趣缺缺。

Josh

How do you break the deadlock?

那你是怎麼打破僵局的呢？

Kenny

I shift the focus to the special functions in the flagship version. Clearly knowing GIO has the ambition to step into the industrial design, our multi-tasking platform in this version is a good cornerstone for them.

我把重點轉移到旗艦版的特殊功能上。我深知GIO想進軍工業設計領域，旗艦版中的多工平台對他們而言是很好的墊腳石。

Josh	Good job, man. Upon hearing this, they will **ponder** the value of our software. <u>But I really wonder how you force their hand in the long run?</u>	做得好。一聽到這句話，他們會去深思軟體的價值。但我更好奇的是你怎麼讓他們提前下單的？
Kenny	I tell them that this software is not available for all consumers in this **phrase**, we only recommend it to the one whom we regard as a distinguished guest.	我告訴他們這套軟體現階段尚未全面開方銷售，我們只先介紹給貴賓。
Josh	What a good sales skill. Feeling being valued, they buy our software.	真是厲害的銷售技巧。由於感到受重視，他們就買單了。

【主管與屬下間】

Between the supervisor and the employee

Adam 亞當	I have heard ABC Company kept being picky to you, so please tell me what is going on. Maybe my point of view can help you solve the problem.	我聽說ABC公司一直在找你碴，所以跟我報告一下確切狀況。或許我的看法可以幫你解決問題。

Carter 卡特	Though ABC Company informed that they received our quotation last week, I am still waiting for their official reply. To **accelerate** the progress, I sent another e-mail to them this morning, but got the feedback that they need more specific **measurement** of the product.	雖然ABC公司上週就告訴我他們有收到報價單了，但我現在仍未受到其正式回覆。未來加快交易進度，我早上再寄出一封電子郵件提醒，但卻得到他們要求更精確產品尺寸的回覆。
Adam	According to my experience, this replay is to ask for more discounts rather than size re-confirmation. Since we have provided a favorable price, we should **yield** nothing to their request. Here I give you two suggestions. One is telling them the quotation will be expired three days later. The other is we have the right to sell this patch of product to other buyer at the same price if the first buyer fail to give the confirmation in time.	根據我的經驗，這樣的回覆根本是在拗打折而不是做尺寸最後確認。由於我們已經提供優惠價，所以不可能同意再降價的要求。這邊我提供你兩個建議。一個告訴他們三天後報價就失效。另一個是說如果買方無法及時給予回覆，賣方有權將此批貨物以相同價格賣給其他買方。

Part 3

【外勤】業務／採購銷售篇

Carter	Since ABC Company has tightened the budget, <u>so I will take the first one to force their hand.</u>Thank you Adam. I am so lucky to have a good boss like you.	由於ABC公司已經緊縮預算，我打算採用第一個方法來迫使他們接受報價。我很幸運有像你這樣的好老闆。
Adam	You are welcome. Now you have found the direction, so try to finalize it soon.	別客氣。既然有處理方向了，就儘快搞定這筆交易吧！

C 對話單字、片語說分明

① **convinced** *v.* 說服

例 To convince the buyer, I find the data made by the authority as the reference.

為了說服買家，我提供權威單位所製作資料作為佐證。

② **premise** *n.* 前提

例 We accept your quotation with the premise of paying by installment.

在可以分期付款的前提下我們接受你的報價。

③ **ponder** *v.* 深思

例 Though the investment is huge in this project, we have to ponder how much the revenue it can generate.

雖然此專案的投資金額甚鉅，但我們要去思考他所能獲取的收益。

④ **phrase** *n.* 階段

例 In this phrase, the source code is only available for senior engineers.

現階段原始碼只提供給資深工程師使用。

⑤ **accelerate** *v.* 加速

例 The function added in this system is to accelerate data categorizing.

新增的系統功能是為了加速資料分類。

⑥ **measurement** *n.* 尺寸

例 Please confirm all the measurement before the shipment.

出貨前請再次確認尺寸。

⑦ **yield** *v.* 讓步

例 Though TGH is our important client, we still yield nothing to their ridiculous request this time.

雖然TGH是重要客戶，但我們對於他們這次離譜的要求絕不讓步。

D 換句話說補一補

With this premise, they show no interest in my recommendation at the beginning.
在此前提下，他們一開始對我的推薦興趣缺缺。

★ **Viewing the purchase with a resistive attitude**, they show no interest in my recommendation at the beginning.

★ **Not prioritizing this purchase**, they show no interest in my recommendation at the beginning.

★ **Regarding this is not essential**, they show no interest in my recommendation at the beginning.

 解析時間

① **Viewing n. with a ... attitude**

解析 Viewing *n.* with a ... attitude意思是「以…的態度看待…」。由於不同處理態度會大大左右事情的結果，因此當你覺得客戶對於交易的態度積極，就可以Viewing this deal with an aggressive attitude, they...，反之則只需把aggressive替換為negative之類具負面意涵的單字。

② **Not prioritizing...**

解析 Not prioritizing... 意思是「未將……列為優先」。如果沒把事情列為優先事項，通常會拖到很久以後才去做。因此當你想表達客戶一再拖延下單，就可以用Not prioritizing this deal, they...來表示。

③ **Regarding ...is not essential**

解析 Regarding...isnot essential意思是「認為…可有可無」。當某人覺得某事可有可無時，最後真的會去做的機會通常很低。因此當你發現客戶對於你的產品推薦意興闌珊時，就可以用 Regarding... is not essential, they... 來表示。

Clearly knowing GIO **has the ambition to** step into industrial design, our multi-tasking platform in this version is a good cornerstone for them.

我深知GIO想進軍工業設計領域，旗艦版中的多工平台對他們而言是很好的墊腳石。

★ Clearly knowing GIO **eagerly want to step into industrial design field**, our multi-tasking platform...

★ Clearly knowing GIO **tend to expand its business coverage to** industrial design, our multi-tasking platform...

 解析時間

① **eagerly want to step into ... field**

解析 eagerly want to step into ... field意思是「急切地想進軍…領域」。此用法中的 step into 表現出從首次嘗試此項目的意涵，因此，當你想表達公司欲進軍新領域時，We eagerly want to step into ... field, so...來表示。

② **tend to expand its business coverage to...**

Part 3
【外勤】業務／採購銷售篇

解析 tend to expand its business coverage to意思是「想把事業版圖擴增至…」。在經營模式上，許多公司當在某個領域站穩腳步後，會嘗試相關的其他領域，以其賺取多利潤。因此，當你想表達這樣多角經營的概念時，就可以用We tend to expand its business coverage to... because...來表示。

Since we have provided a favorable price, we should **yield nothing to their request**.

由於我們已經提供優惠價，所以不可能同意再降價的要求。

★ Since we have provided a favorable price, **no more compromise shall be made**.

★ Since we have provided a favorable price, we should **decline** this request.

 解析時間

① **no more compromise shall be made**

解析 no more compromise shall be made意思是「不應再有任何讓步」。任何一筆交易，買賣雙方都會有其底限。如果超出此範圍，往往寧可破局也不願損及自身利益。因此，當你想表達這樣的立場時，就可以用Since..., no more compromise shall be made來表示。

② **decline...**

解析 decline...意思是「拒絕……」。交易過程中，買賣雙方都只會選擇性接受對方的要求，因此在販售商品的過程中，當你覺得對方的要求非常無理，就可以用Since..., I decline...來表示。

E　非學不可的職場小貼示

　　本對話中有一個名詞叫做favorable price，意思是「優惠價」。這個看起來很感覺意思跟特價差不多的名詞，事實上包含了許多商業意涵在內。

　　在解釋到底有那些意涵前，先來考一下大家歷史。清朝時割地賠款時有提到的最惠國英文該怎麼說呢？答案是the most favorable countries。你會發現當中也出現了favorable這個字。接下來就解釋使用此字的緣由。既然名為「最惠國」，理所當然只會有某幾個國家享有這個權利，所以favorable第一個先表現出排他性。再者，既然有個「最」字，代表所享受優惠是肯定很多。

　　若把最惠國的這些概念套回favorable price，代表該價格非所有客戶皆可享有，另外，這樣的價格通常已經很低，要再降價的空間不大。因此，往後當你說出This is a favorable price, so...這類句型時，若客戶有留意弦外之音，就會知道你表達出這格價格接近底限，要再降價空間不大了。

Unit 23 Take over 接管

 辭彙文化背景介紹

　　如果單看 take 與 over 的個別意涵，take 有「拿取」的意思，over 則可解釋為「從某一邊至另一邊…」。若用數學的方式把意思相加，可以得出 take+over=「把…從某一邊拿到另一邊」的意涵。而東西會換位置，代表在所有權上也可能有所變更，所以 take over 後來也就衍生出「接管」的意思

　　另外，如果仔細思考為何有接管的必要，就會發現十之八九都是壞事。要不就是經營出現狀況，不然就是團隊無法解決問題，又或是離職的業務交接。而當接管一事與我們有所關時，如果做為接管方，就可以用 I will take over...（我要接管…）說明接管的項目或物品為何。若是被接管的一方，...will be taken over by... 是你會用到的句型之一。

看看辭彙怎麼用

【同事間】Between colleagues

Amanda 艾曼達	Kelly told me that she got the **permission** from the graduate school yesterday.	凱莉告訴我她昨天獲得研究所的入學許可了。
Benny 班尼	Congratulations to her. But I remember Kelly didn't apply for the degree program, namely she had to quit, right?	恭喜她。但我記得她並不是申請在職專班,所以換句話說,她得辭職對吧?
Amanda	Yeah. Going back to school to have a further study has been Kelly's **career development** for long, so now her dream comes true. But now Ms. Huang has to **brainstorm** who the best candidate of her position is.	沒錯。再回學校進修是凱莉一直以來想做的生涯規劃,所以她現在美夢成真了。但現在黃經理得思考誰最適合接替這個職位。

Part 3

【外勤】業務／採購銷售篇

Benny	True.Kelly is an outstanding sales representative, because she can always make the **picky** client shut up and place a new order. I can't think of who are qualified in our department to take over her duties.	沒錯。凱莉是很傑出的業務，因為總是有辦法讓挑剔的客戶閉嘴，而且下了新的訂單。我想不出來在我們部門有誰可以接手她的工作。
Amanda	Rumor says that Peggy is the chosen successor. I feel surprised upon hearing this news, but now I think it is a wise decision.	據傳佩姬是內定的繼任人選。剛聽到此消息的時候我很驚訝，但現在想想這似乎是個明智的決定。
Benny	What do you mean by saying this?	為什麼這樣說呢？
Amanda	Though Peggy is green but she has clear thinking. And most important of all, she has a great passion to this job.	雖然佩姬還是菜鳥，但她思路很清晰。最重要的是，她對這份工作有熱忱。
Benny	Let's wait and see whether the rumor is correct or not.	那就讓我們看看謠言是否會成真了！

【主管與屬下間】
Between the supervisor and the employee

Andy 安迪	How do you feel about your performance in the past few months, Charles?	查爾斯，你覺得過去幾個月來你表現如何呢？
Charles 查爾斯	To be honest, disappointed. I get no new order this quarter, so I think I may hear words like "Thank you for your hard working in the past, but here I am sorry to tell you...."	坦白說，很糟。我本季沒有得到任何訂單，所以我想應該會聽到「很感謝你過去的努力，但這邊我必須很抱歉地跟你說…」這類的話。
Andy	Don't be so **negative**. The flaw in our agent policy could be one of the reasons which cause the shrink in the sales figure, so now we are improving it. What I really want to say here is I have asked Lauren to take over the region you are responsible for and now you are in charge of another mature market.	別這麼負面。代理商政策的瑕疵可能是造成業績下滑的原因之一，所以我們現在正努力修正中。這邊我想說的其實是我已經請羅倫接替你所負責的區域，你則換處理另一個成熟市場。

Charles	I feel much relieved now. When you ask me about my feeling toward my performance, losing my job is the thought that comes into my mind.	聽到這我放心多了。當你問我對於自己的表現感覺如何時，第一個閃過腦中的念頭是我要失業了。
Andy	I am not that cruel. Moreover, a horse may stumble on four feet, so I should give you another chance to prove yourself a good sales.	我沒這麼殘忍，況且馬有失蹄，我應該要給你另一個證明自己是優秀業務的機會。
Charles	I deeply **appreciate** your kindness.	我真的很感謝你的寬容。

 對話單字、片語說分明

① **permission** *n.* 允許

例 To get the permission from the authorities, we should submit a related document.
為了當局的許可，我們必須提交相關文件。

② **career development** *n.* 生涯規劃

例 Jane decides to quit because she has another career

development now.

由於已有其他生涯規劃，珍決定辭職。

③ **brainstorm** *v.* 腦力激盪

例 Let's brainstorm to find the way to break the bottleneck we are facing in sales.

讓我們一起腦力激盪一下，找出如何突破銷售瓶頸的方法。

④ **picky** *adj.* 挑剔的

例 Sally can always make picky guests calm down.

莎莉總是有辦法讓挑剔的客人冷靜下來。

⑤ **negative** *adj.* 負面的

例 Don't be so negative, we still have the chance to get this order.

別這麼負面，我們還是有機會拿下這張訂單的。

⑥ **mature** *adj.* 成熟的

例 Since this market has become mature, we can put more resources to make it stable.

由於此市場已成熟，我們可以投入更多資源使其穩定。

⑦ **appreciate** *v.* 感激

例 I really appreciate your help in the program.

非常感謝你在此專案所給予的協助。

D 換句話說補一補

I can't think of who **are qualified** in our team to take over her duties.

我想不出來在我們部門有誰可以接手她的工作。

★ I can't think of who is **the proper candidate in** our team to take over her duties.

★ I can't think of who **are suitable for** taking over her duties in our team.

★ I can't think of any **appropriate successor** in our team to take over her duties.

 解析時間

① **the proper candidate**

解析 the proper candidate意思是「適合的人選」。檢視誰有資格，換個角度看就是在找合適人選。而此用法也透露出符合條件的可能不只一人，要經過比較後才會決定最後人選。因此，當我們在工作上碰到需要推舉人選時，就可以用I think... is the proper candidate來表示。

② **be suitable for**

解析 be suitable for意思是「適合…」。如果從語意上推敲，適合某職位代表該位人選具有該份工作所需的特質。因此，當發現工作上的夥伴適合處理某項任務，就可用Sb. is suitable for...表示。若是某個方法適用某種情況，則可用sth. is suitable for... 說明。

③ **appropriate successor**

解析 appropriate successor意思是「合適的繼承者」。廣義來看，也是在說接手的人要符合某種資格。因此，當你發現同事或是你自己很適合接手處理某項業務時，就可以用I am an appropriate successor to...這一類的句型表示。

But now Ms. Huang has to **brainstorm** who the best candidate of her position is.

但現在黃經理得思考誰最適合接替這個職位。

★ But now Ms. Huang has to **take much time in** findingwho the best candidate of her position is.

★ But now Ms. Huang has to **ponder** who the best candidateof Kelly's position is.

 解析時間

① **take much time in**

解析 spend much time in意思是「花很多時間來…」。當我們需要花時間做某事，就代表這件事情可能很需要動腦。因此，當我們在工作上碰到難題，需要花點時間解決，就可以用We have to spend much time in...這類句型表示。

② **ponder**

解析 ponder意思是「深思」。這個單字表現出不論前因後果，或

是各項條件都被納入考量，因此在概念上也與brainstorm接近。未來在職場上，如果碰到需要仔細思考才能進行下一步的事情，就可以用I need to ponder my next step concerning... 來表示。

A horse may stumble on four feet, so I should give you another chance to prove yourself a good sales.
況且馬有失蹄，我應該要給你另一個證明自己是優秀業務的機會。
★ **Everyone makes mistakes,** so I should...
★ **Life is filled with ups and downs,** so I should...
★ **Even Homer sometimes nods,** so I should...

 解析時間

① **Everyone makes mistakes**

解析 Everyone makes mistakes意思是「人都會犯錯」。在語意上與對話中的馬有失蹄相近，都是要表達犯錯是可以被允許的。因此，當在工作上夥伴有所失誤時，不妨用everyone makes mistakes來表達鼓勵之意。

② **Life is filled with ups and downs**

解析 Life is filled with ups and downs意思是「人生充滿起起伏伏」。此用法雖然沒有直接點出人都會犯錯，但表現出低潮是人生必經階段，因此仍可互做替換。因此，自己或是同事當遇到工作上不順遂時，就可以用這句話作為砥礪。

③ **Even Homer sometimes nods**

解析 Even Homer sometimes nods意思是「人非聖賢，孰能無過」。本用法中的Homer據傳是著名史詩奧德賽和伊里亞德的作者，這邊則作為專家的指稱，用以說明連專家都可能偶有失誤，更何況一般人。因此，往後當同事出錯時，不妨以較寬容的態度看待，用 Even Homer sometimes nods, so you... 這類句型給他或她一些鼓勵。

E　非學不可的職場小貼示

　　第一眼看到policy這個單字，相信大家直覺聯想到這跟政治有關。但事實上，在商業領域中，policy一字的應用十分廣泛，若將其解釋為「方針」就更容易理解箇中巧妙。

　　在商業領域中，舉凡各個面向的大方向，都可以policy合併使用。舉例來說，information security policy指的就是資安方針，代表公司資安的最高準則。因此，根據這樣的邏輯，我們可以類推出investing policy、loaning policy分別叫投資方針與借貸方針。讀完這個小單元後，下次在商業領域中看到policy一字時，千萬別再以為它是在講政治了喔！

Part 4
【外勤】國際貿易
溝通與人事篇

Unit 24 Keep an ear to the ground
注意事情的最新發展

 A 辭彙文化背景介紹

　　若不考慮引申意涵，單看字面我們應該會將此用法翻譯為「把一隻耳朵緊貼地面」。做這樣動作的目的又是什麼呢？就讓我們回到美國西部拓荒時期來抽絲剝繭。

　　在此時期，拓荒者在開拓過程中有許多機會與印地安人接觸，也逐漸學會他們的狩獵與自保技巧。為了確認自己與野獸的距離，印地安人會整個人趴在地上，用耳朵去聽是否有靠近的腳步聲。也因為距離是變動的，稍不留神可能就讓自己身陷危險，因此後來 keep an ear to the ground 後來就引伸出「注意事情的最新發展」的意思。

　　推敲出真正的意思後，往後再進行國際貿易時，由於兩地在地理上有所區隔，更應留意各種要素的變化情況。因此，不論你是要提醒自己掌握脈動，或是告知同事某物料可能會有價格變化，都可以用 keep an ear to the ground before... 來表示。

B 看看辭彙怎麼用

【同事間】 Between colleagues

Mike 麥克	Since there are 60 days left before the shipment, the purchase of new part from AIP in USA is not hurry.	還有60天才出貨，所以想美國AIP買零件的事情還可以先擱著。
Leo 里歐	I strongly suggest you do it early. A **strike** of harbor labor occurred in Seattle last week, paralyzing the import and export in that region. Since the right of labor has been neglected for long, it could just be the **fuse** of large scale strike. What if all harbor labors in west coast fight for their right, the chance is high for us to get no parts before shipment.	我強烈建議你別拖到太晚。上星期西雅圖發生罷工，癱瘓該區的進出口。由於港口工人的權益長期受到忽視，這個罷工可能只是大罷工的導火線。如果所有西岸的港口工人群起捍衛自身權益，出貨前我們可能還拿不到零件。

Part 4

【外勤】國際貿易溝通與人事篇

Mike	<u>I know how serious it would be, so I will keep an ear to the ground.</u> But if my memory serves me right, strike is categorized in **force majeure**. The insurance company shall cover all the lost if we take either Institute Cargo Clause plus with Institute Strikes Clause-Cargo.	我知道其嚴重性，所以會留意罷工的最新情況。但如果我記得沒錯的話，罷工屬於不可抗力因素。如果有保倫敦保險協會貨物保險條款中的任何一款主要險再加上協會罷工險條款（貨物），保險公司就要負擔我們的所有損失。
Leo	Your argument is right in most case. However, now we have known one strike happened, namely the insurance company can explain this event doesn't match the definition of "unexpected".	在多數情況你的論點是對的。但由於我們現在已經知道有罷工的產生，換句話說，保險公司有有將其解釋為不符「不可預期」定義的空間。
Mike	Thank you for your reminding. Not to leave any **uncertainty**, I will place an order today.	謝謝你的提醒。為不產生模糊空間，我今天就先下單。

【主管與屬下間】

Between the supervisor and the employee

Redd 瑞德	According to the schedule, we will carry out the purchase for the second half of this year. However, I have noticed the price of several **raw materials** has a great **fluctuation** in the past two months. Can you give the more specific explanation?	依照時程表，我們即將進行下半年度的採購。但我有留意到過去兩個月來原物料價格的波動甚大，可以跟我詳細解釋一下原因嗎？
Brooks 布魯克	Sure. In terms of corn, the bad weather caused poor **harvest**. Since demands are higher than supplies, the price goes up. When it comes to timbers, the war stops all the export.	關於玉米，天候不佳導致欠收。由於需求高過供給，價格自然攀升。而木材部分則是因為戰爭導致無法出口。
Redd	If the trend continues, the price might go sky high. Have you come up any solution?	如果這樣的趨勢持續，價格都會走高至天價。你有想出什麼對策了嗎？

Part 4

【外勤】國際貿易溝通與人事篇

Brooks	Though bad weather is the act of god, I think we shall pay in a reasonable range. <u>I will keep an ear to the ground and try to find some new candidates in the same time.</u> Because we find it hard to predict when the war will end, we have no alternative but to choose another company to import timber.	雖然天氣不佳屬於不可抗力因素，但價格要在合理範圍內我們才會付款。我會持續留意價格變化，並且找尋合適的新供應商。由於很難預測戰爭何時結束，我們只得尋找其他廠商來進口木材。
Redd	I see. Please report your progress every three days.	我了解了。請每三天跟我回報進度一次。

 對話單字、片語說分明

① **strike** *n.* 罷工

例 Due to the strike in New York harbor, we have to send the part by air.

由於紐約港正處於罷工狀態，我們必須改以空運方式寄出零件。

② **fuse** *n.* 導火線

例 Expanding working hours without overtime pay is the fuse of this strike.

延長工時但卻沒有加班費是本次罷工的導火線。

③ **force majeure** *n.* 不可抗力

例 The delay is caused by force majeure, so we don't have to compensate.

由於延遲是肇因於不可抗力，所以我們不用賠償。

④ **uncertainty** *n.* 不確定性

例 To eliminate the uncertainty, we add many special provisions to the contract.

為了避免有模糊空間產生，合約中加入許多特別條款。

⑤ **raw material** *n.* 原物料

例 Because of the lack of one raw material, we have no choice but to stop the manufacturing of this machine temporarily.

由於其中一項原物料缺貨，我們只能暫時停止製造此機器。

⑥ **fluctuation** *n.* 波動

例 The fluctuation in metal price has been great in the past six months, so I suggest you not to invest this market now.

過去半年來金屬價格起起伏伏，所以我建議你現在先別投資此市場。

⑦ **harvest** *n.* 收成

例 The poor harvest of wheat results in the increase in bread price.

小麥欠收導致麵包漲價。

Part 4

【外勤】國際貿易溝通與人事篇

A strike of harbor labor occurred in Seattle last week, **paralyzing** the import and export in that region.
上星期西雅圖發生罷工，癱瘓該區的進出口。

★ A strike of harbor labor occurred in Seattle last week, **stopping the operation of** the import and export in that region.

★ A strike of harbor labor occurred in Seattle last week, **making the total commodity** import and export in that region **drop to zero**.

★ A strike of harbor labor occurred in Seattle last week, **closing the channel of** the import and export in that region.

 解析時間

① **stop the operation of...**

解析 stop the operation of...意思是「停止⋯⋯的運行」。就商業行為來看，若某個大環節無法運作，整個流程可能就被迫中斷。因此，當你發現自己或同事在進行過國際貿易是遭遇此狀況，就可以用 ...stop the operation of..., so we have no choice but... 來表示。

② **make the total N drop to ...**

[解析] make the total N drop to ... 意思是「使整體……下降至……」。做國際貿易時,各項因素的變化程度遠比國內貿易難掌控,有些因素可能會因為某事件就突然大幅下滑,當你遇到這種情況時,就可以用 ...make the total *n.* drop to ... 來表示。

③ **close the channel of**

[解析] close the channel of 意思是「關閉…的管道」。若要貿易,就必須適當的管道,因此當通路因故無法發會作用,整個交易也會被迫停擺。因此,當你遭逢這樣的衝擊時,就可以用 ...close the channel of..., postponing the ...of ... 來表示。

But if my memory serves me right, strike is categorized in force majeure.

★ But **to my knowledge**, strike is categorized in force majeure.

★ **As I know**, strike is categorized in force majeure.

 解析時間

① **to one's knowledge**

[解析] to one's knowledge 意思是「根據…的認知」。商場瞬息萬變,很多時候事情的演變往往未照預期,甚至與既有概念相違背。因此,當我們真的實際遭遇時,就可以 Sth. should ...to my knowledge, but it ... 來表示。

② **As sb. know**

> **解析** As sb. know意思是「就…所知」。與上述用法相似，本用法同樣強調想法與實際狀況的差異。因此，當實際狀況與過去既有想法衝突時，你就可以用As I know, ...should... 來表示。

> However, I have noticed the price of several raw materials **has a great fluctuation** in the past two months.
> 但我有留意到過去兩個月來原物料價格的波動甚大，可以跟我詳細解釋一下原因嗎？
> ★ However, I have noticed **the price of several raw materials wasn't stable** in the past two months.
> ★ However, I have noticed the price of several raw materials **kept going up** in the past two months.

 解析時間

① **The N of N wasn't stable in the past...**

> **解析** The *n.* of *n.* wasn't stable in the past...意思是「……的…在過去……內並不穩定」。由於貿易本身就存在很多不確定性，當你想表達這樣的起伏時，就可以用The *n.* of *n.* wasn't stable in the past...來表示。

② **kept v. ing**

> **解析** kept *v.* ing意思是「持續……」。作為一名貿易人員，掌握市場趨勢是不可或缺的。因此，當你發現任何一項指標或價格有持續上升或下降的趨勢，就可以用...keep going up/down in the past...來表示。

E 非學不可的職場小貼示

本單元對話中出現的 Force Majeure 與 Act of God 意思是「不可抗力」，是個我們常掛在嘴邊，但對其確切內容一知半解的法律與商業用語。

就範圍來看，不可對抗的類別又分為自然力量與社會力量。自然力量指的是天災，例如水災、風災。社會力量指的是罷工、戰爭、或是政策。

而既然叫做不可抗力，一定包含無法與之對抗這個面向。但單憑這點，還無法為法商界接受。不可抗力形成的客觀因素還包含不可預見與不可避免。不可預見指的是無法事先得知，換句話說，如果能預知，就不算不可抗力。舉例來說，雖然天氣具有不可預測性，但如果出發前已經發布警報，仍執意出航，就等同違反不可預見。而不可避免則指即使採取避難措施仍難以避免。也就是說如果可避免但卻沒有積極作為，例如颱風來了，船隻可以入港避難但船長卻選擇留在外海，這就有違不可避免。

當上述三個要素都成立，就構成不可抗力。透過上述的簡單解釋，往後在貿易過程中談論到如何處置不可抗力時，你就不會在一知半解了。

Part 4

【外勤】國際貿易溝通與人事篇

Unit
25 **Get the upper hand** 佔上風

 辭彙文化背景介紹

　　如果單看字面，你可能一下子整理不出這個用法的語言邏輯，但如果說這個用法跟我們玩過的遊戲有關，要搞懂就簡單得多了。

　　很多人認為此慣用語源自於你我小時候可能都玩過一個遊戲。這個遊戲就是兩個人同時握住一根棍子的底部，看誰先握到棍子的頂端就獲勝。由於雙方是在同一位置出發，先到頂端等於先掌握局面或是有利位置，因此後來 get the upper hand 就引申出「佔上風」的意思。

　　此慣用語除了可以用在人與人談判外，也可表達自己做決策的過程，例如 my emotiongets the upper in the decision making this time。因此，不論是要表達某人取得主導權或是某項要素成為優先考量，都可以使用 get the upper hand。

B 看看辭彙怎麼用

【同事間】Between colleagues

Kate 凱特	After sending the **inquiry** to the pocket list of this purchase, how's the progress now, Jill?	吉兒，向本次採購的口袋名單詢價過後，目前進度如何呢？
Jill 吉兒	The unit price that PYT, MNC, and HDG offer has few differences, but the payment terms are poles apart. PYT requests 100 percent T/T in advance, while MNC accepts credit. HDG is the only one with the option of installment.	PYT、MNC、HDG 開出的單價都差不多，但付款條件就差很多。PYT要求出貨前全額電匯，而MNC接受刷卡。HDG是唯一可以分期的。
Kate	It seems HDG is the top choice because we don't have to pay in **lump sum**.	看來HDG是最佳選擇，因為不用一次付清。

Jill Upon hearing this, I know you are not that experienced in business negotiation. The sum of this purchase is great, so the three candidates are all eager to get this order. Utilizing such **psychology**, we can ask for more discounts. As a result, I send an e-mail to an individual candidate stating that we have more than one choice to them all. Now, PYT offers 10 percent discount, MNC **deducts** the freight, and HDG offers one more year warranty. <u>We get the upper hand all the time in this deal</u>.

聽到你這樣說，就可以看出你在商業談判上還是生手。由於本次採購金額甚大，三個廠商都很希望拿到訂單。利用這樣的心理狀態，我們可以要求更多折扣。因此我各寄一封郵件給個別廠商，內容講的都是我們有不只一個選擇。現在PYT願意打九折，MNC免運費，PYT延長一年保固。在本交易中，我們始終都佔上風。

Kate I never think of this aspect. Jill does teach me a lesson. Next time I will keep an eye on the slightest psychological change in seller or buyer so that we get the whip hand for the most time.

我從沒想到這個部分說！吉兒你真的替我上了一課。下次我會更注意買方或是買方最細微的心態變化，好讓我們能夠主導交易。

【主管與屬下間】

Between the supervisor and the employee

Darren 戴倫	Surprisingly, the horizontal alliance wins an **unprecedented** success. Since all the participant regards this cooperation an experiment, none of us thinks of the settlement of profit. Now we have to deal with the most sensitive issue—margin distribution with our two foreign partners. Wesley, do you have any suggestion concerning this thorny issue?	令人驚訝的是本次異業結盟空前成功。由於所有參與者都視本次合作具實驗性質,沒人考慮到利潤如何分配。現在我們得處理最敏感的議題—如何與兩個外國合作夥伴分享利潤。衛斯理你對於這個燙手山芋有任何建議嗎?
Wesley 衛斯理	The more profit the better, so no one will compromise unless the either of the other two propose an argument which strong enough to convince the rest. <u>To get the upper hand in this negotiation, we need to point out that we are owner of the know-how in this special project.</u>	利潤當然是越多越好,所以沒有人願意妥協。除非其他兩方中的任一方提出一個足以說服所有人的強勁論點。為了要在本次協商中占上風,強調我們是此次特別計畫關鍵技術的擁有者是必要的。

Part 4

【外勤】國際貿易溝通與人事篇

Though channel and marketing are crucial, the program can't hit the market without the core technology. By emphasizing this point, the chance is high for us to get the lion's share.

雖然通路跟行銷都很重要，但以技術為本才能轟動市場。強調此點可讓我們獲得最多的利益。

Darren Your assumption sounds reasonable. In your opinion, what the maximum should we ask for while what is the bottom we have to stick to?

你的推論聽起來很合理。就你看來，最大值應該要求多少，應該堅守的底限又是多少？

Wesley 60 percent is a proper value. This figure is above an half, politely indicating we are the ruler in the league. The minimum shall be 51 percent. If the amount we can get is lower than that, it means we lose the dominating position.

百分之六十是很恰當的數值。這個數字超過一半，委婉地表示我們是這個聯盟的領導者。最低值應該是51，如果能夠獲得的利潤低於此限，代表我們失去主導地位。

Darren Very **insightful** analysis. Good job Wesley. I will apply your argument when I have the meeting with their boss.

非常有深度的分析。衛斯理，做得好。我與其他兩間公司老闆開會時，會採用你的論點。

對話單字、片語說分明

① **inquiry** *n.* 詢價

例 To estimate the total expense, we send the inquiry of parts to ALK.

為了要預估總花費，我們向ALK進行零件詢價。

② **lump sum** *n.* 一次付清的總額

例 If we pay in lump sum, the discount is 25 percent.

如果一次付清，可以打七五折。

③ **psychology** *n.* 心理狀態

例 Knowing the psychology of the buyer can help us get the upper hand in the negotiation.

理解買家心態有助於讓我在談判時居於上風。

④ **deduct** *v.* 扣除

例 For the consumers who purchase three items a time, the freight will be deducted.

消費者只要一次購買三件，就可以享受免運費的優惠。

⑤ **unprecedented** *adj.* 前所未有的

例 The crossover products win an unprecedented success.

跨界商品獲得空前成功。

Part 4 【外勤】國際貿易溝通與人事篇

⑥ **know-how** *n.* 關鍵技術

例 Owning the know-how allows us to take the lead in the market.
掌握關鍵技術可以讓我們領先業界。

⑦ **insightful** *adj.* 有深刻見解的

例 Your analysis is very insightful because you lead us to see this event from a different aspect.
你的分析非常有見解，因為你帶領我們從不同面向看這件事。

D 換句話說補一補

It seems HDG is the top choice because we don't have to **pay in lump sum**.
看來HDG是最佳選擇，因為不用一次付清。

★ It seems HDG is the top choice because we **can pay by installment**.

★ It seems HDG is the top choice because we don't have to **pay off**.

 解析時間

① **pay by installment**

解析 pay by installment意思是「分期付款」。Installment

指的就是分期付款中的一期，若前方再加上monthly或
seasonally這類副詞，就可更加詳細說明每隔多久付款一
次。因此往後若想表達是否可以分期，就可以用Could I pay
by installment? 來表示。

② **pay off**

解析 pay off意思是「付清」。由於介系詞off帶有「消除……」的
意涵，因此pay off指的就是付完這次之後，所有款項都結
清。理解當中的邏輯後，往後要表示一次支付，就可以用pay
off來替代pay in lump sum。

Upon hearing this, I know **you are not that experienced in
business negotiation**.
聽到你這樣說，就可以看出你在商業談判上還是生手。

★ Upon hearing this, I know **you are green in business
negotiation**.

★ Upon hearing this, I know **you have much to learn in
business negotiation**.

 解析時間

① **you are green in...**

解析 you are green in... 意思是「你在……方面還是新手」。在商
業談判上，從分寸拿捏恰當與否，就能看出是老手還新手。
因此，當你覺得同事的判斷有問題，就可以用From..., I can
tell you are green... 來提醒他出錯的關鍵在哪。

② **you have much to learn in...**

解析 you have much to learn in意思是「你在……要學習之處還很多」。此用法也是委婉提醒某人的判斷或是行為不夠深思熟慮，因此當在商業談判中，若你覺得別人的處理手段不夠成熟，就可以用Since...., you have much to learn in...來表示。

By emphasizing this point, the chance is high for us to **win the lion's share**.

強調此點可讓我們獲得最多的利益。

★ By emphasizing this point, the chance is high for us to **get the most benefit**.

★ By emphasizing this point, the chance is high for us to **profit from the negotiation**.

★ By emphasizing this point, the chance is high for us to **be the winner in this negotiation**.

 解析時間

① **get the most...**

解析 get the most...意思是「獲得最多的……」。在商場上，當上了談判桌，目標就是為自己公司爭取最大利益、優勢等。因此當你認為做了某事後，可以達到此效果，就可以用By..., we can get the most...來表示

② **profit from...**

解析 profit from... 意思是「從……中獲利」。與客戶協商的最終目的就是在雙方都同意的前提下，互取最大利益。因此當你發現某個方法可以讓我方得利，就可以用 we can profit from... if.... 來表示。

③ **be the winner in...**

解析 be the winner in... 意思是「成為……的贏家」。當進行商業談判過後，一定會得利與失利的一方，因此當你覺得我方在過程中佔了上風，就可以用 we are the winner in... 來表示。

E 非學不可的職場小貼示

　　在本單元中，出現 the lion's share 這個慣用語。單看字面，會將其理解為「獅子的那一份」，那獅子拿到的部分跟其他部分又有何差別呢？

　　原來這個用法是源自於伊索寓言。在故事中獅子將所有動物的獵物都占為己有，由於獅子是萬獸之王，其他動物無法與之競爭，因此獅子的獵物數量就居所有動物之冠。根據此典故繼續衍生語意，當某人在某項競爭或是分配中取得最多優勢，現在我們就習慣會用 lion's share 來表示。

Part 4

【外勤】國際貿易溝通與人事篇

Back to square one
回到原點

A 辭彙文化背景介紹

Square的意思是方格，所以從字面翻譯的話，整個慣用語的語意就是「回到一號方格」。那回到這個位置有甚麼特殊意義嗎？接下來讓我從足球賽的播報來向各位說分明。

假設有看過足球賽轉播的話，都知道足球場面積非常大，在看到的到畫面的情況下，有時觀眾都可能會弄不清楚球員位置，更不用說是沒有畫面的收音機轉播了。為了要服務收聽廣播的觀眾，後來主播習慣就將足球場化分成幾個方格區塊，只要說出其代號，就可以大致知道位置。由於一號方格就是場中央開球的地方，當雙方球員再次來到這個位置，就好像比賽又重新開始一次，因此back to the square one就衍生出「回到原點」的意思。

此慣用語最常用來指稱做了諸多努力，但最後卻沒有太多進度的窘境，因不論是在談判上產生僵局或是整個計畫泡湯，都可以用Now we go back to the square one來表示。

看看辭彙怎麼用

【同事間】 Between colleagues

Jason 傑森	How's progress in the sales of the inspection **instrument** to Peter& Thomas'?	要賣給Peter& Thomas's的檢驗儀器有進展了嗎？
Chris 克里斯	No progress at all. <u>To be honest, now we almost go back to the square one.</u>	完全沒有。老實說，我們現在幾乎回到原點了。
Jason	How come! All the specifications are confirmed, so I really wonder what is the cause of this deadlock?	怎麼會！所有的規格都已確認，所以我真的很想知道形成僵局的原因？
Chris	It's about **maintenance**. According to the company policy, we bear all the cost of the replacement during the warranty but the seller shall support full transportation fees if they ask for on-spot repair. However, Peter & Thomas' want us to **bear** 50 percent since they buy so many instruments a time.	是關於維修。根據公司方針，保固期內我們承擔所有替換成本。但如果買方要求現場維修，就需負擔相關人員所有的交通費用。

Part 4

【外勤】國際貿易溝通與人事篇

I shall not break the rule, but also I do want to get this order. What can I do, Jason.

Jason It is a Catch-22 because Peter & Thomas' won't place the order if you obey the principle, but you violate the regulation if you compromise. In my opinion, the only solution is to report the **dilemma** you are facing to the managing level.

但 Peter & Thomas's 表示因為他們此次購機數量眾多，要我們自付一半交通費。

這也太讓人進退兩難了。如果你遵守公司規範，Peter& Thomas'就不會下單；如果你選擇跟Peter& Thomas's妥協，就違背公司規定。所以在我看來，最好的解決方式就是向上呈報，讓長官知道你所處的困境。

【主管與屬下間】
Between the supervisor and the employee

Leo 里歐 Have you reached a consensus with ABC Company in the payment terms of this deal?

你有和ABC公司在付款條件上達成共識了嗎？

Ben 班 Not yet, or I should say I go back to the square one.

還沒，或是該說又回到原點了。

Leo What do you mean by saying this?

這麼說的意思是？

Ben	Not considering the exchange difference, ABC finds that they need to 5 percent more to us now due to the **appreciation** of USD. To make this carelessness, they ask for the price **reduction**.	沒考慮到匯差，ABC公司發現它們現在因為美金升值要多付我們百分之五的總額。為了要彌補此大意之舉，他們要求減價。
Leo	Being a businessman, you should have the common sense that exchange rate is a fluctuating value. ABC's request is way too ridiculous. We can't compromise in this case. Have you come up with any otherway re-initiate the negotiation?	身為生意人，你就應該有匯差是浮動值的基本常識。ABC公司的要求簡直無理取鬧，所以我們這次絕不能妥協。你有想出如何以其他方式重啟協商嗎？
Ben	Using the spared key chains to act as the transform of discount sounds feasible. The chain is well-design, so ABC can use it as the free gift to their customers.	贈送我們多的鑰匙圈來當作另外一種型態的折扣或許可行。因為設計精良，他們可以再拿去送客戶。

Part 4

【外勤】國際貿易溝通與人事篇

① **instrument** *n.* 儀器

例 To know the more specific composition of the compound, you should use this inspection instrument.

為了要得知此複合物的組成，你應該使用此檢測儀器。

② **maintenance** *n.* 維修

例 We chose not to buy this car because of its high maintenance fee.

我們選擇沒有購買這款車是因為其維修費甚高。

③ **bear** *v.* 負擔

例 Since this damage is caused by the Act of God, we don't have to bear the repair expense.

由於損害肇因於不可抗力，我們無須負擔任和維修費用。

④ **dilemma** *n.* 困境

例 To escape from the dilemma, we could compromise a little in price.

為了突破困境，我們願意在價格上稍微讓步。

⑤ **appreciation** *n.* 升值

例 We pay less in this deal due to the appreciation Euro.

因為歐元升值，所以我們的實際支付額變少。

⑥ **reduction** *n.* 減免

例 Since the deliveryis delayed, the seller offers a 15 percent price deduction.

由於出貨延遲，賣方給我們八五折優惠。

⑦ **common sense** *n.* 基本常識

例 Using hard currency to reduce the inflation is a common sense.

使用強勢貨幣來降低通膨的影響是一種基本常識。

 D 換句話說補一補

All the specifications are confirmed, so I really wonder **what is the cause of this deadlock**?

所有的規格都已確認，所以我真的很想知道形成僵局的原因？

★ All the specifications are confirmed, so I am really curious **why the negotiation is ceased temporarily**?

★ All the specifications are confirmed, so I really wonder what is **the barrier in commutation**?

解析時間

① ...is ceased temporarily

解析 ...is ceased temporarily意思是「……暫時停止」。當談判碰到瓶頸，雙方的意見交換可能就會暫時中斷。因此當你想表達這種因故停止的情況，就可以用...is ceased temporarilydue to...來表示。

③ the barrier in...

解析 the barrier in...意思是「……的障礙」。在談判桌上，如果雙方對於某向利益或原則都不肯讓步，就會影響整體進展。因此，當你想表達某事物會造成此狀況時，就可以用...is the barrier in...來表示。

It is a Catch-22.
這也太讓人進退兩難了。
★ It is a **dilemma**.
★ It is **an unsolvable problem**.

 解析時間

① dilemma

解析 dilemma意思是「困境」。與difficulty不同，dilemma除了表現出此事具困難度外，還有那種這樣做也不是，那樣做也不是的無奈感。因此，當你在談判或銷售時遇到這種窘境，就可以用The dilemma I am facing is...來表示。

② **...is an unsolved problem**

解析 ... is an unsolvable problem意思是「……是個無解的問題」。無解的問題往往肇因於問題本身就充滿矛盾，導致於你在努力都無法找出解答。因此，當你覺得某一事件根本就鬼打牆，就可以用 ... is an unsolvable problem 來表示。

 E 非學不可的職場小貼示

　　Catch-22的意思是「22號軍規」，出自於同名長篇小說。故事背景設定在二戰時美軍所駐軍的一個小島，由於指揮官不停要求飛行員出任務，到後期很多人都因內心過於恐懼，意圖閃避。若要不出任務，軍醫告知飛行員只要你的狀況符合22號軍規即可。22號軍規內容是只要證明你發瘋，並由本人提出申請，即可暫停執勤。但只要有人申請，就代表他知道任務有危險性，所以等同沒發瘋。

　　由於22號軍規就像是看的到卻用不到的福利，因此後來就其借代為進退兩難的困境。往後不論是在談判或是業務執行上碰到這種讓你不知如何是好的情況時，就可以用Catch-22來表示。

Part 4 【外勤】國際貿易溝通與人事篇

Unit 27 Ace up one's sleeve / Hold all the aces / Ace in the hole 握著王牌

A 辭彙文化背景介紹

在解釋這個用語之前，要先跟講從袖子與撲克牌的關係說起。如果你愛看有關博奕的電影的話，會發現當中的老千幾乎都是穿著長袖服飾玩牌。其實如果仔細想一下，長袖可以藏牌、換牌或動其他手腳而不容易被察覺，但如果是短袖，就很難做到。而玩牌時，除了大老二是二最大，多數的撲克遊戲Ace都是最大牌，因此把Ace偷藏在袖子理，快要輸的時候就可以趕快偷天換日來翻轉頹勢。

按照上述的邏輯，get ace up ones sleeve的字面語意就是「把Ace放到袖子裡準備出牌」。在打出這張牌後，由於戰局可能截然不同，因此後來就引伸為「準備把預留的王牌拿出用」，當初作弊的意涵已逐漸淡化，重點放在翻轉局面。理解這層意涵後，往後當在生意往來上出現狀況，但我方握有改變情況的關鍵因子時，就可以用we get ace up ours sleeve表示。

B 看看辭彙怎麼用

【同事間】Between colleagues

Lee 李	How's the progress in the deal of the commercial computer with ABC Company?	賣給ABC公司商用電腦的那筆生意如何了？
Olivia 奧莉維亞	I have received the quotation with Lucas' signature last week, but I am waiting for the **deposit** now.	我已經收到有盧卡斯簽名的報價單，但還沒收到訂金。
Lee	I feel shocked about that, because ABC Company is famous for its **efficiency**. Do you find the possible reason?	我很驚訝，因為ABC公司向來以高效率著稱。你有找出可能的原因了嗎？
Olivia	The payment term could be the key factor.The **consensus** we have reached is 30 percent deposit before shipment and the down payment should be paid within 7 days working day after arrival of the goods. I guess he goes back on his word now.	付款條件可能是關鍵因素。我與盧卡斯達成的共識是出貨前付百分之三十的訂金，收到貨品後的七個工作天內付尾款。我想盧卡斯現在可能改變主意了。

Part 4

【外勤】國際貿易溝通與人事篇

Lee	All computers have been assembled, so it seems we may face a great loss if ABC Company changes their mind.	所有電腦都已經組裝好了，所以如果ABC公司改變主意，我們可能會面臨鉅額損失。
Olivia	Don't worry. I have got ace up my sleeve, because one of **provisions** in this quotation indicates that the seller has the right to sell this patch to other buyers if the buyer fails to pay the deposit five days prior to the scheduled shipping date. Now ABC Company only has two days left. Moreover, this patch is all popular models, so finding another purchaser is easy.	別擔心，我早留一手了，因為這份報價的有一個條款內容是：「如買家未在預計出貨日的五日前支付訂金，賣家有權將此批貨物買給其他買家。」現在ABC公司剩兩天可以付款。此外，這批電腦都是熱賣款，所以不用擔心找不到新買家。
Lee	Good job, Olivia. This provision can help us remain invincible in this deal.	做得好，奧莉維亞。此條款讓我們在這筆生意上立於不敗。

【主管與屬下間】

Between the supervisor and the employee

Owen 歐文	How's the performance of our agent PKL in the past one year, Jose?	荷西，代理商PKL去年的整體表現如何呢？
Jose 荷西	To be frank, not very good. It had a sales peak in Q1 but has been dropping very sharply ever since until Q3. Fortunately, the sales finally **bounce** back a little in Q4. The overall sales figure didn't reach the expected goal.	坦白說，不是很好。第一季時有銷售高峰，但在那之後就一路下滑到第三季末，第四季才有些許回升。整體銷售數字沒有達到預期目標。
Owen	Such performance is still acceptable as a new agent, because what I really care is whether they are capable to expand the **coverage** of our product.	做為一個新代理商，這樣的表現還勉強可以接受，因為我最在意的是它們有沒有能力拓展公司產品的市場覆蓋率。
Jose	What if PKL still makes no improvement in the coming year, do we set any penalty for this?	如果PKL明年還是沒進步，我們有訂立任何處罰條款呢？

| Owen | I have got my ace up sleeve about this. Let's take a look of the termination part in the contract. Article 3 indicates that the licensor has the right to **terminate** the contract, if the license fails to reach the sales goal for the consecutive two years. PLK has one more year to prove itself. Once PKL fails, another successor is in. | 關於這點我早就留一手了。讓我看一下合約裡關於契約終止的部分，當中第三條的內容就是如果被授權者連續兩年未到達授權者所設立的銷售目標，則授權者有權終止該合約。PKL還有一年可以證明自己的實力。如果失敗了，就會有新的代理商接手。 |

 對話單字、片語說分明

① **deposit** *n.* 訂金

例 The deposit of the deal shall be paid two days prior to the shipping date.

本次交易的訂金需於出貨日前兩日支付。

② **efficiency** n. 效率

例 UHG is famous for its high efficiency in the market.

UHG在業界以高效率著稱。

③ **consensus** *n.* 共識

例 To reach the consensus in the investing issue, Tom and I are invited to attend this meeting.

為了要在投資議題上達成共識，湯姆與我受邀參加此次會議。

④ **provisions** *n.* 條款

例 This provision is written for preventing a malicious price cutting.

此條款是為了避免惡意削價產生。

⑤ **bounce** *v.* 反彈／回升

例 Our performance finally bounces back in Q4 due to the financial aid from our partner.

在商業夥伴的金援下，我們的業績終於在第四季回升。

⑥ **coverage** *n.* 涵蓋範圍

例 To expand the coverage of our product in the world, we enter Korea's market this year.

⑦ **terminate** *v.* 終止

例 Once the buyer violates any article written in the contact, the seller has the right to terminate this deal.

D 換句話說補一補

I guess he **goes back on his word** now.
我想盧卡斯現在可能改變主意了。

★ I guess he **has changed his mind.**
★ I guess he **feel regret for his decision** now.
★ I guess he **tend to break the promise** now.

 解析時間

① **has changed one's mind**

解析 has changed one's mind意思是「某人已經改變想法」，在概念上與go back on one's word相近，都是表達現在之前說的話不算數。

② **feel regret for sb.decision**

解析 feel regret for his decisions意思是「對自己做出的決定感到懊悔」。會有這樣的行為，代表想法已經改變，覺得自己當初不該這樣答應對方。

③ **tend to break the promise**

解析 tend to break the promise意思是「試圖違背承諾」。人會想違背承諾就是因為後悔了。因此，當我們在職場上要強調自己立場前後一致時，可以用I won't break the promise表示。發現對方打算反悔時，則可使用...tend to break the promise加以說明。

This provision can help us **remain invincible in** this deal.
此條款讓我們在這筆生意上立於不敗。

★ This provision can help us **get the upper hand** in this deal.

★ This provision can help us **has the floor** in this deal.

★ This provision can help us to **have an ace in hole**in this deal.

 解析時間

① **get the whip hand**

解析 get the whip hand意思是「掌握優勢」。在交易中掌握優勢，最後得利的機會相對較高，不太可能吃虧。因此，當自家公司或是你在與客戶交易中取得主導權，就可以用I/Our company get the whip hand in .... 來表示。

② **has the floor**

解析 has the floor意思是「擁有發言權」。在會議中，當某人有發言權時，其他人包含會議主席都不可干擾，此時發言人最大。當我們在與客戶協議價格時取得上風時，就好像在會議中拿到發言權，因此也可以用I has the floor in this deal with...表示。

③ **have an ace in hole**

解析 have an ace in hole意思是「尚有王牌在手」。由於這個條款是為了防止代理商擺爛而設計，因此如果代理商表現良好，就只是備而不用。這樣的邏輯與王牌只用在特殊情況不謀而

合。因此，在與客戶談判中如果發現情勢被扭轉，該出招反擊時，就可以用 I still have an ace in the hole 表示。

What if PKL still **make no improvement** in the coming year, do we set any penalty for this?
如果PKL明年還是沒進步，我們有訂立任何處罰條款呢？

★ What if PKL still **can't have any progress** in the coming year, do we set any penalty for this?

★ What if PKL still **have a weak performance** in the coming year, do we set any penalty for this?

★ What if PKL still **fail to achieve the goal** in the coming year, do we set any penalty for this?

 解析時間

① **can't have any progress**

解析 can't have any progress 意思是「沒有任何進步」，在語意上跟「沒做出任何改善」相近，都是要表達沒有讓人驚豔的表現。因此，當我們發現合作夥伴在工作上一直沒進展時，就可以用 ...can't have any progress in... 來表示。

② **have a weak performance**

解析 have weak performance 意思是「表現不佳」。從實務面來看，表現不佳基本上也就很難有有所進步。因此當要表達某個工作進行的不順利，或是某個合作夥伴表現有待加強，就可以用 ...have weak performance 來表示。

③ **fail to achieve the goal**

解析 fail to achieve the goal意思是「無法達成目標」。一般來說，無法達標的原因之一就事是表現不夠好。從廣義來看，兩者可以互做替換。因此，當自己或是夥伴表現未達標準時，就可以用 ...fail to achieve the goal來表示。

 E 非學不可的職場小貼示

在本單元對話中，有出現terminate這個單字，意思是「終止」，大家對這個單字最深的印象可能來自電影魔鬼終結者（Terminator），但事實上此單字是商用與法律英文中常見的單字之一。

電影裡的終結者是要終結敵人，在商業領域的終結多數指的是合約。由於人都是自私的，合約的內容最後一定會對某一方較有利，當對方違反某項雙方合意的項目，合約的效力即刻終止。這個部分就是所謂的契約終止（Termination）部分。主導的一方會在此設定對自己有利的條件，因此未來在簽約時，若我方非主導方，一定要針對此部分內容仔細閱讀，才不會因為一時的懶惰而被對方吃的死死的。

Hit someone between the eyes 讓人印象深刻

Unit 28

A 辭彙文化背景介紹

單就字面來看，10個人中大概有9個半會覺得這跟打架有關，因為如果朝某人兩眼之間攻擊，不論是徒手或使用武器，光用想的就覺得被打的人應該會痛到不行。

從這個畫面繼續延伸，當一個人遭受如此攻擊時，當下會有最直接的反應，事後也會留下深刻印象，有時候還會因為這樣的衝擊突然理解某事，因此現在 hit someone between the eyes 已用來指稱「讓人印象深刻」，或是「使人突然想通」。

理解語意後，往後在與客戶交涉過程中，因為某事而突然想通知前所無法解決的問題，或是覺得某人的舉只想法讓你驚艷，就可以用 ...hit me between the eyes 來表示。

B　看看辭彙怎麼用

【同事間】**Between colleagues**

Emma 艾瑪	After listening Ben's presentation, I find one thing strange. ABC Company has more than one model which meet our need, but Ben only focuses on type 207.	在聽完班的簡報後，有件事讓我覺得有很奇怪。就是ABC公司明明有不只一項產品符合我們需求，但班只著重在207型上。
Vivian 薇薇安	Type 207 is one of their bestsellers, so I don't think anything goes wrong. Maybe you are too **sensitive**. But a little bird told me that ABC will release a new series in Q4, could it has something to do with today's briefing?	207型式他們的暢銷商品之一，所以我不覺得有任何怪異之處。或許是你太敏感了。但據可靠消息指出，ABC公司第四季會推出一系列新產品，這會跟今天的簡報有關嗎？
Emma	<u>Your words hit me between the eyes</u>. I also hear the rumor that the new models will be the **flagship** version of type 207. My assumption here is Ben uses an indirect way to launch a **clearance sale**.	你的話讓我恍然大悟，因為我也聽說新款會是207型的旗艦版。這邊我會推測班是用了一個迂迴的方式在出清存貨。

Part 4

【外勤】國際貿易溝通與人事篇

285

Vivian	Upon connecting all the **clues** we have found, knowing whether the product we buy which about to be out of date or not is crucial.	當把所有發現的線索串聯起來，我覺得有必要去了解我們所購入的品項是否即將成為過時商品。
Emma	Not to reveal our intent, I would ask the question like"what if you release the upgrade version in the near future, what can you do for us?"to test Ben.	為了不要意圖太明顯，我會問班類似這樣的問題：「如果近期有推出升級版，你可以替我們做什麼？」
Vivian	Good idea. I will ask him this question in the e-mail.	好主意。我會在電郵中問他。

【主管與屬下間】

Between the supervisor and the employee

| Jessica 潔西卡 | The model we need is not available until six months later, so we have to find the alternative. Do you have any suggestion concerning this situation? | 我們需要的型號要6個月後才有貨，所以得個替代方案才行。對此你有任何建議嗎？ |

Ann 安	As I know, there are some other models could serve the same function **in general**. In terms of the customized design, using the part with **compatibility** to upgrade could be the solution.	就我所知，還有其他型號功能大致也相同。至於客製設計的部分，使用具相容性的零件來升級也許是個解決之道。
Jessica	<u>Your words hit me between the eyes</u> because I don't think of using part upgrade to shorten the waiting time. But the questions here are what if the seller is reluctant to sale the parts alone or the cost of this adjustment is high. But anyway, we can convey this though to them first.	你的論點讓我印象深刻，因為我從來沒想到用零件升級去縮短等待時間，但這邊會碰到幾個問題。一是萬一賣家不肯單賣零件，二是這樣的調整費用很高。但說真的，我們可以先告知他們此想法。
Ann	Yeah. Since the replacement occupys a small **portion** in the whole design, the cost shall be affordable as long as the seller is willing to provide such service in my opinion.	沒錯。由於需更換的部分只佔總體設計的小部分，就我看來只要賣家肯提供這樣的服務，價格應該是不會太高昂。
Jessica	Agree. Later, I will send an e-mail ask for the quotation of the model and replacement respectively.	同意。等下我會寫信請求賣家針對所需型號與替換品分別報價。

Part 4

【外勤】國際貿易溝通與人事篇

C 對話單字、片語說分明

① **sensitive** *adj.* 敏感的

例 Sam doesn't mean to cheat in this deal. Maybe you are too sensitive.

本次交易山姆不是有意要欺騙，或許是你太敏感了

② **flagship** *n.* 旗艦

例 If you have a higher budget, our flagship version is your top choice.

如果你預算較高，我們的旗艦版是你的首選。

③ **clearance sale** *n.* 清倉拍賣

例 We will launch a clearance sale soon, so you have to wait for a while if you want to save some money.

我們即將舉行清倉拍賣，如果想省錢的話，就需要再稍微耐心等候。

④ **clue** *n.* 線索

例 From the clues we have found, dumping in this market is the ultimate goal of ABC Inc.

從我們發現的線索看來，在此市場進行傾銷是ABC公司的最終目的。

⑤ **in general** *ph.* 一般來說

例 The unit price of this material is between 9 to 15 USD in general.

這種物料的單價一般來說在9到15美金之間。

⑥ **compatibility** *n.* 相容性

例 Considering the compatibility, we choose this software.

考量到相容性的問題，我們選擇此款軟體。

⑦ **portion** *n.* 部分

例 The sales of the clothing accounts for a small portion of our business.

服飾的銷售僅佔我們事業版圖的一小部分。

D 換句話說補一補

Type 207 is one of their **bestsellers**, so I don't think anything goes wrong.

27型式他們的暢銷商品之一，所以我不覺得有任何怪異之處。

★ Type 207 is one of **the most popular products**, so I don't think anything goes wrong.

★ Type 207 is **a hot item to their customer**, so I don't think anything goes wrong.

Part 4

【外勤】國際貿易溝通與人事篇

解析時間

① **... is one ofmost popular items**

解析 ...is one of the most popular items意思是「…是最受歡迎商品之一」。當某一商品很受歡迎，其銷售狀況自然好。因此，當你覺得某項商品的銷售情況很好，就可以用 ...is one of most popular items來表示。

② **a hot item to ...**

解析 a hot item to ...意思是「是…的熱銷商品」。由於hot不只可以用來表達溫度上的高溫，也可以用來表達產品或事情的被接收度很好，因此當你想表達某項商品現在很搶手，就可以用 N. is a hot item to...來表示。

In terms the customized design, using **the part with compatibility** to upgrade could be the solution.

至於客製設計的部分，使用具相容性的零件來升級也許是個解決之道。

★ In terms the customized design, using the part which **serves the same function** to upgrade could be the solution.

★ In terms the customized design, using the part which **applies the same development concept** to upgrade could be the solution.

解析時間

① **serve the adj. function**

解析 serve the *adj.* function意思是「有…的作用」。在採購時，難免碰到所需產品缺貨的情況，若某項其他產品在功能或性質上與原來所需相似，我們就可以用…serve the same function with… 來表示。

② **apply the ... concept**

解析 apply the....concept意思是「採用…的概念」。就設計的角度來看，若最初發想的源頭概念相近，最後的成品就可能相似，因此當你想表達兩個產品具有很高相似程度時，就可以用…apply the same concept with… 來表示。

 E 非學不可的職場小貼示

　　對話中所提到的clearance sale指的就是我們所熟悉的清倉拍賣，有的時候也可以用close out sale表示，因為兩者的目標都是達到零存貨。但要特別注意的事，除非是因為店面要搬遷、或是廠商真的倒閉了，才建議使用close out sale表示。因為出清這次後，該店或該廠商就不會再營業了。反之，其他出清舊商品的特賣，就建議用clearance來表示。

Clinch a deal 成交

A 辭彙文化背景介紹

　　Clinch是一個讓人非常有畫面的動詞,意思是「用釘頭敲彎的方式把…釘牢」。仔細想想,某樣東西經過這種方式固定後,要移動就變得非常困難,而這樣的不易變動性,也就是clinch a deal真正意涵的來源。

　　用榔頭或槌子將釘頭敲彎做固定,目的是為了避免受固定物有在鬆動的可能性,那如果今天我們要固定的是一樁交易,又代表什麼意思呢?做交易最怕的就是有一方反悔或是臨時追加條件,趕快拍板定案,就可以避免節外生枝。

　　順著這樣的邏輯推演,在何種狀況下交易不會再有變動?答案是成交的時候。所以clinch the deal的意思就是「成交」,或是口語所說的「搞定這筆交易」。理解用法之後,往後在交易完成後,你就可以用I have clinched the deal來表達了。

B 看看辭彙怎麼用

【同事間】Between colleagues

Julia 朱莉亞	Has TTT Company determined the computer model they would like to buy?	TTT 公司有決定出這次要購買那一型的電腦了嗎？
Tony 東尼	Not yet. Their sales Ann just informed me that most of the total of the suitable model **exceeds** the **budget** maximum, so they may **turn to** other brand.	還沒。TTT 的業務安告訴我說多數他們覺得適合的型號，總價都超過預算上限，所以可能會轉而購買其他品牌。
Julia	I am not surprised at all. Buying 100 computers at a time costs a lot, so I may ask for a discount like that if I were her. What kind of discount you would like to offer this time?	這在我意料之中。一次買 100 台電腦的總金額不是個小數目，所以如果我是安的話，也會這樣拗折扣。那這次你預計給多少折扣呢？

Part 4

【外勤】國際貿易溝通與人事篇

Tony	In most case, we won't sell the product to our customer by the list price in such amount, so 15% at most. It is a good **bargain** if anyone can get this price in this amount in the market, so I assume TTT will accept this favor.	在多數情況下，當客戶如此大量採購時，我們不會依定價販售，最多可以打到八五折。綜觀業界，在此數量下可以獲得此折數已經實屬難得，因此我覺得TTT會接受此優惠。
Julia	I see. Hope you can clinch the deal soon.	我知道了。祝你早日搞定這筆交易。

【主管與屬下間】

Between the supervisor and the employee

Kevin 凱文	One month has passed, Have you clinched the deal with KTP, Carl?	已經1個月過去了，你到底把車賣給KTP了沒，卡爾？
Carl 卡爾	Almost. After making the comparison, KTP finds that our price is the most competitive. The reason why they haven't placed the order is because of their special need in coating and passenger's **privacy**.	快要了。經過比價之後，KTP發現我們的價格最低。為何還沒有下單是因為在烤漆與乘客隱私上有特殊需求。

Kevin	Doesn't they know we provide a customized service?	難道他們不知道我們有提供客製化服務嗎？
Carl	That is the key of hesitation because they regard such service as the **privilege** of **luxury** car buyer. Upon knowing we can change the coating and enhance the privacy with an affordable charge, they are so shocked. After the final reconfirmation, they will pay the deposit by T/T.	這就是猶豫的原因，他們認為客製服務是高級車買主的特權，當他們知道調整烤漆與增強乘客隱私，只需可支付一個大家都負擔得起的價格時，都非常訝異。在與我們做過最後確認後，就會電匯訂金。

C　對話單字、片語說分明

① **exceed** *v.* 超過

例 The cost of repair exceeds our expectation, so we choose to buy a new one instead.

由於維修費用超過預期，我們選擇直接在買新的。

② **budget** *n.* 預算

例 Finding no budget for the replacement, we have no choice but to stop the operation of this machine.

由於沒預算可以替換零件，我們只得暫停運作這台機器。

③ **turn to....** *ph.* 向⋯尋求⋯

例 Since the capital needed in this investment is huge, we turn to shareholders for the financing.

由於本次投資所需資金甚鉅，我們向股東們尋求融資。

④ **bargain** *n.* 買賣

例 It is really a good bargain to buy this machine at this price.

能用此價格買到這台機器非常划算。

⑤ **privacy** *n.* 隱私

例 The greatest strength of this system is to keep your privacy safe.

這套系統的最大優點就是能夠保障你的隱私。

⑥ **privilege** *n.* 特權

例 10 percent off for all items is the privilege of our VIP.

我們的VIP獨享所有品項八折的優惠。

⑦ **luxury** *adj.* 奢華的

例 The price of this phone is doubled due to its luxury decoration.

奢華的裝飾讓這支手機價格翻倍。

換句話說補一補

Has TTT Company determined the computer they would like to buy?
TTT公司由決定出這次要購買那一型的電腦了嗎？

★ **Has TTT Company confirmed** the model of the computer they would like to purchase this time?

★ **Does TTT Company decide the model** of the computer they would like to purchase this time?

 解析時間

① **Has/have sb. confirmed...**

解析 Have sb. confirmed...意思是「某人是否已確認……」。就一般交易程序而言，當雙方皆表示確認，就需為此決定負責。因此，當你要詢問對方是否已確認過所有交易環節，就可以用Have you confirmed...來表示。

② **Do/does sb. decide the n. of...**

解析 Do sb. decide the *n.* of...意思是「某人是否已完成……」。做生意有時候也很講究程序，要按環節慢慢來。因此，當你想詢問對方是否已完成某個程序時，就可以用Do you finish the *n.* 來表示。

Part 4 【外勤】國際貿易溝通與人事篇

That is the key of hesitation because they regard such service **as the privilege of luxury car buyer**.

這就是猶豫的原因，他們認為客製服務是高級車買主的特權。

★ That is the key of hesitation because they regard such service **as exclusive to** luxury car buyer.

★ That is the key of hesitation because they deem **only the luxury car buyer can enjoy such service**

 解析時間

① **...is exclusive to sb...**

解析 ...is exclusive to sb.意思是「……為某……所專屬」。特權指的就是少數人所擁有的權利，換個角度看，就是排除多數人所得來。因此，當你覺得某項優惠應當只開放給某些客戶時，就可以用 ...is exclusive to sb.來表示。

② **only sb. can enjoy...**

解析 only sb. can enjoy...意思是「只有某……可以享有……」。為了禮遇消費額較高或是特殊的顧客，廠商往往會提供一些特殊優惠給此族群，當你想表達某人享有這種特權時，only sb. can enjoy...,so you can...來表示。

E 非學不可的職場小貼示

　　本單元對話中，出現了bargain這個單字，名詞動詞皆可，在商用對話中，是個非常好用的字彙。若應用在買賣上，a good bargain指的是「划算的交易」。Bargain with sb.意思是「與某人討價還價」。bargain on...還可表達「在…上達成協議」。

　　理解了bargain的各種用法後，往後當你想表達划算時，就不會只有cheap、cost effective這個字彙。表達協商時，也不會每次都只能用negotiation，達成共識也不見得都要講reach a consensus on。既然bargain用途這麼廣，讀完這個單元後就趕快想辦法記住這個單字吧！

Part 4

【外勤】國際貿易溝通與人事篇

Unit 30 Meet somebody halfway
向某人妥協

 A 辭彙文化背景介紹

　　一看這個慣用語，大多數人一定會將其理解為「在半路遇到某人」，因為我們習慣把halfway用在人的相遇上。但這邊將這種空間的對峙延伸應用至想法的對抗上。

　　如果把一件事比喻為一個有限的空間，一個人的想法當成一個實際存在的物體，想法的推演就是物體的移動。而當兩個人的想法交會時，可能出現兩種情況，一是其中一方退讓，另一方前進，二是兩方都堅守住自己底線，未讓對方越雷池一步。第二種情況其實也可以解讀為有條件同意對方，也是本用法的真正語意「向某人妥協」。

　　理解語意後，往後當某人提到meet somebody halfway，你就不會答腔說「我也很久沒碰到…」，讓自己貽笑大方，而是懂得繼續詢問到底在哪些部分做出讓步。

看看辭彙怎麼用

【同事間】 Between colleagues

Oliver 奧利佛	How's our business of **screws** in Mexico?	我們在墨西哥的螺絲銷售情況如何？
James 詹姆士	Quiet good. Last week, CVB sent an inquiry of 60,000 screws. Though we **sacrificed** some profits in this trade, we still won the orders.	很好。上週CVB來信詢問6萬顆螺絲的價格。雖然此次交易犧牲掉一些利潤，但贏得後續的訂單。
Oliver	What do you mean by "sacrifice some profits"?	犧牲掉一些利潤指的是？
James	Since the margin of a screw is not high, we provide a **fixed** discount of 10 percent of every 10,000 pieces purchase. In other words, the favor won't change with the total amount. However, we meet CVB halfway in this purchase.	由於一顆螺絲的利潤並不高，所以我們提供每1萬顆就打9折的固定折扣。換句話說，折扣數不會因為總量提高而增加。但這次我跟CVB妥協了。
Oliver	It is the very first time you compromise, so can you tell me why?	這是你第一次讓步，可以告訴我原因嗎？

Part 4
【外勤】國際貿易溝通與人事篇

James	CVB's international sales manager gives me an oral **commitment** that CVB will place an order like this time every quarter this year, so I provide another 5 percent discount as the feedback.	CVB 的國貿經理口頭承諾我他們公司本年度會每季下一次數量跟本次相同的訂單，所以我就再給百分之五的折扣。
Oliver	I see. Anyway, this favor wins more business opportunities for us. Good job.	我了解了。畢竟這樣的優惠替我們贏得更多商機。做得好。

【主管與屬下間】
Between the supervisor and the employee

Anderson 安德森	Have you finalized the licensing of our smart phones to LLL in their country, Joe?	喬，LLL 有取得在該國販售我們智慧型手機的授權了嗎？
Joe喬	Yes, everything is settled eventually, but I have to say LLL is tough.	有，一切終於就定位，但我必須說 LLL 的態度真得很強硬。
Anderson	Tough? Can you give a specific explanation?	強硬？可以給我清楚一點的說明嗎？

Joe	For all of our **agents**, we provide them a favorable price to leave more room for profits. Not feeling satisfied with the discount alone, LLL asks for free gifts to attract consumers or they will turn to other brands. <u>I never accepted such a request in the past, but I meet LLL halfway this time.</u>	對於所有的代理商，我們都給予優惠價來擴大其利潤空間。但不甘於只享有優惠，LLL要求免費贈品來吸引消費者，否則就轉投其他品牌的懷抱。我過去從沒答應這樣的要求，但這次我妥協了。
Anderson	How come? I guess you see the whole thing in a bigger picture.	為什麼呢？我猜你是用更宏觀的角度看這件事。
Joe	You are right. Considering LLL is the largest **communication** company in this region, I promise LLL to randomly **package** a crossover key chain inside the accessory kits. Since the gifts are all in sponsorship, no cost is added.	沒錯。考慮到LLL是當地最大的通訊商，我承諾會在配件盒中隨機包裝聯名鑰匙圈。因為這些鑰匙圈是贊助的，所以成本沒有增加。

Part 4

【外勤】國際貿易溝通與人事篇

Anderson	What a wise decision. Such strategy can create a buzz among consumer, because they have no idea who will get it until the moment they tear the seal. Most people may assume LLL gets the upper hand, but I think you control everything instead.	很睿智的決定。這樣的策略會在消費者間引起話題，因為要到拆封那一刻才知道誰有拿到鑰匙圈。多數人會認為LLL佔了上風，但我覺得你反而掌握了一切狀況。
Joe	You really know me well. Using zero cost to win a stable partnership is definitely cost effective.	你真得很了我。在不增加成本的前提下贏得一個穩定的合夥關係，何樂而不為呢！

C 對話單字、片語說分明

① **screw** *n.* 螺絲

例 Though a screw is tiny, it plays a important role in our product.

螺絲雖小，但卻在我們的產品中扮演重要角色。

② **sacrifice** *v.* 犧牲

例 Though this notebook is thin, it won't sacrifice the

efficiency.

這款筆電雖然薄，但並未犧牲其效能。

③ **fixed** *adj.* 固定的

例 To avoid incompatibility, we use a fixed parameter in all of our products.

為避免不相容的情況產生，我們所有產品都使用同一組參數。

④ **commitment** *n.* 承諾

例 This agreement is based on the oral commitment few days ago.

這份合約是以前幾天的口頭承諾為基礎。

⑤ **agent** *n.* 代理商

例 Currently, we don't have any agent in this region

我們於此區目前尚無代理商。

⑥ **communication** *n.* 通訊

例 ABC is one of the leading communication companies in the market.

ABC公司是通訊業的龍頭之一。

⑦ **package** *v.* 包裝

例 All of our product will be properly packaged before shipment.

我們的產品出貨前都會仔細包裝。

Part 4

【外勤】國際貿易溝通與人事篇

D 換句話說補一補

> However, we meet CVB halfway in this purchase.
> 但這次我跟CVB妥協了。
>
> ★ However, we **accept CVB's request with a certain premise** in this purchase.
> ★ However, we **compromise with CVB** in this purchase.

 解析時間

① **Sb. accept one's request with....**

【解析】 Sb. accept one's request with....意思是「某人在……的前提下接受某人的要求」。在商業談判上，為了顧全大局，有時候會有條件讓步，而這樣的妥協就可以用 we accept one's request with... 來表示。

② **compromise with...**

【解析】 compromise with...意思是「與……妥協」。在買賣過程中，雙方如果一直僵持不下，對彼此都不利。

> Since the gifts are **all in sponsorship**, no cost is added.
> 因為這些鑰匙圈是贊助的，所以成本沒有增加。
>
> ★ Since **we don't pay for this gift**, no cost is added.
> ★ Since **the sponsor cover all the expense of the gifts**, no cost is added.

解析時間

① **we don't pay for ...**

解析 we don't pay for... 意思是「……不是由我（方）出錢」。就成本概念來看，若某項產品或資源不是由我方出資，就不會計算在成本內。因此，當你想表達這種零成本的狀況時，就可以用 Since we don't pay for..., it... 來表示。

② **Sb. cover all the expense of ...**

解析 Sb. cover all the expense of... 意思是「……負擔……的所有開銷」。同樣就成本的概念來看，所有開銷的總和就是成本。因此，當你想敘明這個基本商業概念時，就可以用 Sb. cover all the expense of..., so... 來表示。

E 非學不可的職場小貼示

　　Oral commitment 只的是口頭承諾，是商用對話中常出現的用語，但使用時要注意以下幾點，才可以保障自身與公司的權益。就法律面來看，除非口頭承諾的當下有錄音，否則當事後其中一方反悔，另一方就必須負起舉證的責任（the burden of proof）。由於有時候越是簡單的是越難舉證，因此口頭上達成共識後，建議儘快將其文字化，以保障雙方權益。

Unit 31 Take (time) off / Have (time) off 休假

 A 辭彙文化背景介紹

當我們看到 take off 這個用法，一定想到會是「拿走」的意思。那如果今天被拿走的東西是「時間」，代表什麼意思呢？

當我們拿走一樣的東西，在某範圍內原來這樣東西的位置就空下來了，所以除非有事先告知，否則別人會找不到這樣東西。根據這樣的邏輯，如果我們拿走某個工作時段，又沒告訴別人的話，要找我們處理公事的人也會撲空，所以 take 時間 off 就是你我都熟悉的休假。

但休假的形式有好多種，到底要怎樣說才對，以下針對時否詳述事由說明。假如你固定某天休假，由於已成定案，沒有說明原因的必要，就可以用 I take every 時間 off。但如果要請事假、病假這類的假別時，本用法因為需要補述原因，建議只保留動詞 take，後面加上事由 +leave，例如 I would like to take a sick leave 意思就是我明天想請病假。

B 看看辭彙怎麼用

【同事間】Between colleagues

Tina 提娜	Since the deadline of the project is approaching, I work overtime everyday since this Monday. If necessary, I may need to work this weekend. I am **overwhelmed** by such a heavy workload.	由於專案的截止日快到了，我從星期一起天天加班。如果有必要的話，這個週末也得進公司。我快受不了這樣的工作負擔了。
Fiona 費歐娜	Me, too. Our manager, Peter has different thoughts all the time, so the report has been revised for countless times. What I have done in the past few days is deleting, re-writing.	我也是。彼得經理總是有新想法，所以報告已經不知道修正幾次了。我這天都在刪除與重寫間徘徊。
Tina	If possible, I would like to leave all my duties aside to have a vacation now.	如果可能的話，現在好想放下工作去渡假喔！
Fiona	Come on, Tina. Stop **daydreaming**. Unless you are terminally ill, I assume no leave will be **permitted** before the due date of this project.	吼！提娜，別做白日夢了！除非生重病，不然我看在專案完成前誰都別想請假。

Part 4

【外勤】國際貿易溝通與人事篇

Tina	I know, but I still want to **complain**.	我知道,但就還是很想發發牢騷。
Fiona	Let's hang in there. I remember you tell me that you still have two PTOs left, so you can use it to relax yourself.	我們一起再撐一下吧!我記得你有跟我說你還剩兩天特休,所以可以善用這兩天去好好放鬆。
Tina	True. I will definitely take a two-day off when the project is done.	沒錯。我絕對會在專案完成後請兩天假來休息。

【主管與屬下間】
Between the supervisor and the employee

Tom 湯姆	Morning, Brad, are you free to talk now?	早安,布萊德,現在有空說話嗎?
Brad 布萊德	Sure. What is going on, Tom?	當然有,湯姆你有什麼事要跟我說呢?
Tom	It is about my paid time off. I have promised my kid to take them to Disney Land this summer vacation, and next Tuesday and Wednesday is a good timing because my wife is also free during that period of time.	是關於特休。我跟我的小孩保證今年暑假會帶他們去迪士尼樂園玩,二下星期二與星期三是個很好的時間點,因為那兩天我的妻子也休假,

| | So I was wondering if I can take a two-day off on the dates I just mentioned? | 所以我想請問是否那兩天我可以請假呢？ |

Brad I am a father, too, so I can imagine how frustrated your kid would be if I refuse your application. However, the deal with TYB still has many problems, so you have to find a **deputy** to take over your duties during your vacation.

我也已經當爸了，所以很了解如果拒絕你的申請，你的小孩會有多失望。但現在與TYB的交易仍存在許多問題，所以我要你找到職代在你休假時接管你的業務。

Tom Do you mean if I can find a person to deal with all the tasks concerning with TYB next Tuesday and Wednesday, then I can have two-day leave to take my kids to **go around**?

你是說只要我到人在下星期二與星期三幫我代為處理與TYB有關的所有事情，我就可以帶小孩去玩了嗎？

Brad Right. Considering the workload, I suggest you to ask Ryder or Cindy. If either of them accepts your request, please ask him or her to sign on your application form and I will stamp on it to finish the **procedure**.

沒錯。考量到工作負擔的問題，我建議你找萊德或辛蒂。如果任何一個人答應你的請求，就拜託他/她在你的申請單上簽名，然後我再蓋章完成整個請假手續。

Part 4

【外勤】國際貿易溝通與人事篇

① **overwhelmed** *v.* 使…受不了

例 I feel overwhelmed by the marathon meeting.
馬拉松式的會議令我難以招架。

② **daydream** *v.* 做白日夢

例 What we need is a partial suggestion, so please stop daydreaming.
我們需要有建設性的意見，所以別在那做白日夢了。

③ **permit** *v.* 許可

例 Since this program may consume many budgets, I think it won't be permitted by the president.
由於此計畫可能消耗很多預算，我想總裁應該不會表示許可。

④ **complain** *v.* 抱怨

例 Susan complained to me about the bad attitude of the new employee.
蘇珊像我抱怨新人的不良態度。

⑤ **deputy** *n.* 代理人

例 Dan is my deputy when I take a day off.
我休假時，丹是我的職代。

⑥ **go around** *ph.* 四處晃晃

例 I take one day off tomorrow, so I will do nothing but go around.

我明天休假，所以我除了四處走走外，打算其他什麼事都不做。

⑦ **procedure** *n.* 程序

例 Though the project is very urgent, you still have to finish all the procedure.

雖然此專案很緊急，但還是要照程序來。

 D 換句話說補一補

I am **overwhelmed** by such a heavy workload.
我快受不了這樣的工作負擔了。
★ I **am fed up with** such a heavy workload.
★ I **have had enough of** such a heavy workload.
★ I **can't bear** such a heavy workload.

 解析時間

① **be fed up with**

解析 be fed up with意思是「受夠了……」，當中的fed可用說明某人已經受不了某事所帶來的影響，因而有想要擺脫的想法。在職場上，有壓力在所難免，但如果壓力大到真的難以承受，就可以用I have fed up with the pressure of...來表示。

② **have had enough of**

(解析) have had enough of意思是「已經受夠……」，當中的enough加強了到達臨界點的意思，超過此極限後，可能就會出現不良影響。在職場上，只出一張嘴的人其實不再少數，若實在無法忍受她/他的頤指氣使，就可以用I have had enough of her...來表示。

③ **can't bear**

(解析) can't bear意思是「無法再忍耐」，在語意上與上述用法都是再強調已經超過最大忍受值。當我們在工作時，若遇到自己實在無法忍受的情況，想要與之對抗或是索性退縮逃避，就可以用I can't bear..., so I...來表示。

If possible, I would like to **leave all my duties aside** to have a vacation now.

如果可能的話，現在好想放下工作去渡假喔！

★ If possible, I would like to **shelve my duties temporally** to have a vacation now.

★ If possible, I would like to **have an deputy of my duties** to have a vacation now.

★ If possible, I would like to **escape from the reality** to have a vacation now.

解析時間

① **shelf my duties temporally**

解析　shelf my duties temporally意思是「暫時擱置業務」。當我們被工作壓力壓得喘不過氣時，就會出現先稍微休息一下，等下再繼續的想法。而這樣的想法就可以用I would like to shelf my duties temporarily to...

② **have an deputy of my duties**

解析　have an deputy of my duties意思是「找到一個職務代理人」。在職場實務上，若你的職務有人代理，主管就比較願意准假，你也就可以去放鬆或是處理私事。因此，下次找到職代要向主管請假時，就可以用I have a deputy of my duties, so could Itake a leave to...來表示。

③ **escape from the reality**

解析　escape from the reality意思是「逃離現實」。在職場上，所謂的現實指的就是乖乖工作，因此逃離現實就是不用工作放假去。所以未來當我門工作到筋疲力盡，但卻又放不了假時，就可以I would like to escape from the reality to..., but...的句型來發發牢騷，舒緩心情。

I am a father, too, so I can imagine how frustrated your kid would be if I **refuse your application**.

我也已經當爸了，所以很了解如果拒絕你的申請，你的小孩會有多失望。

★ I am a father, too, so I can imagine how frustrated your kid would be if **your application is denied by me**.

★ I am a father, too, so I can imagine how frustrated your kid would be if **I didn't permit your application**.

★ I am a father, too, so I can imagine how frustrated your kid would be if **you can't have a leave on that period of time**.

 解析時間

① **Sb's application is deniedby...**

　解析　your application is denied by... 意思是「申請遭⋯拒絕」。如果請假被主管拒絕，換句話說就是沒得休假。在職場上，主管拒絕你的申請是很常見的情況，因此幫我們碰上時，就可用 My application is denied by... 來表示。

② **I didn't permit your application**

　解析　I didn't permit your application 如果「我不許可你的申請」。主管如果不讓申請審核通過，員工的請假程序就沒完成，等於無法休假。在職場上，遇到此種情況時，從自身的角度表達時，就變成 my application is not permitted by...。

③ **you can't have a leave on that period of time**

【解析】 you can't have a leave on that period of time 意思是
「你無法再那段時間休假」。若某員工無法在有需求的時段休
假，即代表長官不准假。這樣的句型架構除了用在請假上，也
可以替換成別的需求。以出差為例，如果長官不准，就會說
you can't have business trip on that period of time。

 E　非學不可的職場小貼示

　　對話中所出現的 deputy 一字，意思是「職代」，但相
信大家在公司職務架構圖中也看過此單字，因為 deputy 也
有「副手」的意思。透過下段的簡單解釋，相信各位就能理
解箇中原因。

　　以總經理為例，對應的單字叫 general manger，副總
經理對應的單字就叫 deputy general manager。若從業
務職掌的角度看，何時副總經理會有實權？就是總經理因為
出差無法或其他因素導致親自行使職權的時候。因此副總其
實總經理的職務代理人。

　　理解了這層意涵後，以後看到客戶的職稱前有 deputy
一字，就會知道她或他可能是是某個部門的副主管了。

Leader 036

會賺$的貿易英文
用 Smart 慣用語跟老外這麼說，賺$有效率

作　　者	邱佳翔
發 行 人	周瑞德
執行總監	齊心瑀
企劃編輯	饒美君
校　　對	編輯部
封面構成	高鍾琪

內頁構成	華漢電腦排版有限公司
印　　製	大亞彩色印刷製版股份有限公司
初　　版	2016 年 01 月
定　　價	新台幣 349 元
出　　版	力得文化
電　　話	(02) 2351-2007
傳　　真	(02) 2351-0887
地　　址	100 台北市中正區福州街 1 號 10 樓之 2
E - m a i l	best.books.service@gmail.com
網　　址	www.bestbookstw.com

港澳地區總經銷	泛華發行代理有限公司
地　　址	香港新界將軍澳工業邨駿昌街 7 號 2 樓
電　　話	(852) 2798-2323
傳　　真	(852) 2796-5471

國家圖書館出版品預行編目資料

會賺$的貿易英文：用 Smart 慣用語跟老外這麼說，賺
$有效率/ 邱佳翔著.-- 初版.-- 臺北市 ：力得文化，
2016.01　面 ； 　公分.-- (Leader ; 36)
ISBN 978-986-92398-6-8(平裝)
1.商業英文　2.慣用語

805.123　　　　　　　　　　　104027865